THE ESSENCE OF FICTION

The Essence of Fiction

A Practical Handbook for Successful Writing

MALCOLM McCONNELL

W·W·NORTON & COMPANY

NEW YORK·LONDON

Copyright © 1986 by Malcolm McConnell. *All rights reserved*. Published simultaneously in Canada by Penguin Books Canada Ltd, 2801 John Street, Markham, Ontario L3R 1B4. Printed in the United States of America.

FIRST EDITION

The text of this book is composed in Gael, with display type set in Novarese Book and Optima. Composition and Manufacturing by the Haddon Craftsmen. Book design by Marjorie J. Flock.

Library of Congress Cataloging-in-Publication Data
McConnell, Malcolm.
    The essence of fiction.

    1. Fiction—Technique.   I. Title.
PN3355.M35   1986   808.3   85-28531

ISBN 0-393-02306-0

W.W. Norton & Company, Inc., 500 Fifth Avenue, New York, N.Y. 10110
W.W. Norton & Company Ltd., 37 Great Russell Street, London WC1B 3NU

1 2 3 4 5 6 7 8 9 0

Contents

A Personal Note from
the Author

THERE ARE a number of excellent creative writing books available today. I found more than a dozen on the shelves of a university bookstore when I began to research this project. So, it could be argued that there's a certain coals-to-Newcastle redundancy in my wanting to produce yet another "definitive" handbook for the aspiring fiction writer, whether he be a college student or a would-be professional who works weekends on a novel or a collection of short stories.

Nevertheless, I offer this book with the confidence that what I have assembled here will, in fact, complement, not attempt to supplant, the existing body of creative writing literature. This confidence stems from the goals I have set and the experience I draw upon at the outset.

In chapter one, I discuss at length that perennial academic bugaboo, "Can you really teach writing?" I've taught enough people how to write fiction to state without hesitation that, yes, indeed, writing is a teachable skill, just like driving a car, flying an airplane, tap dancing or picking pockets, for that matter. But there is, I think, implicit in the perennial question another, unspoken and more germane point: "Can you really teach someone to write *well*, with inspired grace, with genius?" In short, can any creative writing book, teacher, class or workshop take normal human clay as raw material and turn out a contemporary Shakespeare, Coleridge, Charlotte Brontë, Hemingway, Thomas Pynchon or Joan Didion?

Drawing on my seventeen years' experience as a professional writer and a teacher of writing, I can also answer the implicit question. No, definitely not. No book or class, no matter how well structured, can produce a literary genius. As confident as I am in my own abilities to teach, I would never presume that my book could help create a great writer. But I would suggest that this book could help *train* such a writer. We must never forget that every highly skilled individual, every virtuoso, learned that skill somewhere, acquired it from some *external* source in his life. Unlike the ants and the bees, we do not have programmed into our DNA the ability to produce instinctively works of great and complex beauty.

Having made that obvious point, let me state the obvious corollary. No virtuoso—literary, musical, dramatic or medical—ever reached that pinnacle of skill ignorant of the basic elements of his craft. A great brain surgeon first studies pre-med chemistry and physics, then, in medical school, biochemistry and anatomy, microbiology . . . and so forth, until the day, perhaps fifteen years into his apprenticeship, the surgeon lays the cool scalpel edge on the moist, white tissue of the living brain.

So it is with writers. No novelist ever wrote a complex and emotionally moving work of fiction who had not first mastered such elemental skills as writing effective dialogue or maintaining consistent and relevant point of view and narrative voice. Good professional writers, like good brain surgeons, are careful craftsmen. Don't get me wrong, I'm not suggesting that they are *cautious*—far from it. Being careful does not imply a lack of venturesome spirit. I'm simply pointing out that the mature, professional virtuoso has spent an intense apprenticeship. He has command over all the fundamental elements of his profession. He may not be sure of the outer limits, of what can be accomplished in a surgical procedure or in the chapter of a novel, but he knows the pitfalls, the problems he must avoid. Here's another truism, but one pertinent to my case: they don't pay professionals to make mistakes. *Ergo,* one definition of a professional craftsman: a person who has learned sufficient skills to avoid or correct mistakes.

Let's think for a moment about the creative writing classroom. On one side of the seminar table we have the professional, hopefully a true virtuoso—the writer as teacher. Across the table we have the amateur writers, the students. All too often, in my experience, the educational transaction that occurs here is incomplete . . . that is, the teacher is unable to teach very much, and the students do not learn any practical craft that will actually help them as aspiring writers. All too often, by default, these sessions become diffuse *literature* discussions, not writing workshops.

The analogy that occurs to me is of the crusty old brain surgeon standing before a room of pre-med students, holding up the detailed technical report on an operation and asking the students what they think of it. Replace the doctor with the fiction workshop writer who flourishes a Chekhov story and calls for the opinions of his class.

What the hell *should* they think of it? The pre-med students don't know a hemostat from a serum electrolyte, and the kids in the writing seminar wouldn't recognize point of view if it bit them on the ankle. "I think it's interesting," replies the eager boy in the fatigue jacket. The girl beneath the Farah Fawcett mane states, "I liked it better the second time I read it."

Interesting? You *liked* it? Who cares? What I want to know is this: How does Chekhov integrate dialogue and physical action within setting and conflict situation? Does the point of view remain consistent throughout the story? Why does it shift, what's the *purpose,* from the writer's perspective? *Huh? What?*

I don't know what you mean. Nobody ever taught us about setting. (We haven't gotten to hemostats or serum electrolytes yet, Doctor.)

Every honest, self-respecting creative writing teacher should read "The Emperor's New Clothes" each night before he goes to bed. Then, on rising in the morning, ask himself this question: Am I really teaching my students a craft? Am I helping them form skills that they can apply to the practical problems of writing? Or, like the fawning Mandarin courtiers who praised the Emperor's non-existent robes, do the members of my workshop apply the irrelevant standards of literary criticism to student stories, then exacerbate the problem by interjecting purely subjective personal opinions?

All too often, in my experience, creative writing textbooks and the teachers who use them fall victim to what I call the Emperor's New Clothes Fallacy. These teachers use finished literature, usually classic novels and stories—perhaps the works of Chekhov—as models for student discussion, and, in theory, I guess, student emulation. This is, I feel, like asking the nineteen-year-old pre-med student to comment on the neurosurgery report, then, *somehow* to absorb craft by osmosis from this report and replicate the feat of medical virtuosity.

I hope that this book avoids the worst of those errors and fallacies.

If you want literary models (and we all do, we *need* them) go to the library. But, if you want to discover what dialogue really is, how it works in a piece of fiction, and, more importantly, what dialogue can and cannot accomplish in your fiction, then read this book. If you're curious about the potential value of one physical setting vis-à-vis another, if you wonder about the best way to move a character from point A to point B without needless and clumsy exposition, then read this book.

In short, if you want to learn how fiction, effective narrative storytelling, actually *works*, from the perspective of the writer, not that of the literature student, read this book.

The models I employ here are not Chekhov or Hemingway or Margaret Atwood. I use student stories to prove my points: the work of amateurs just like the readers of this book. Moreover, I do not limit my examples to finished, polished student fiction. Instead, I lay out student *draft* fiction, with all its clumsy knobs and pimples, for you to examine, then lead you, the amateur writer, through the logical, unavoidable work of rewriting, the drafting process: the only way truly effective narrative is ever written.

To protect the privacy of the student writers, and also to save them some embarrassment, I have changed the names of certain authors and melded several drafts of certain stories into one version. In this manner, an earlier generation's "mistakes" can help a new generation of writers learn professional habits.

In the course of learning this set of professional habits, you will pass through an abbreviated apprenticeship, maybe in as brief a period as one college semester. Don't kid yourself; you will not have absorbed all of it, or even most of it, in that short a time. This book is not intended to function that way. Rather, I am writing a handbook, a practical guide that you can re-read as your career and level of skills progress. Ten years from now, when you're in the middle of your second novel and you're having trouble with the third-person narrative voice, I'd like this book to be there to serve as a guide.

So that the book will work both as a theoretical primer and a practical handbook, I have written the sections and chapters with a different intensity and scope. The chapters of Part I are densely detailed, replete with fundamental principles—a kind of basic training for fiction writers. Parts II and III are seemingly less crammed with fact, and their more open form makes them more accessible for use as a practical day-to-day handbook.

Writing, they say, is a lonely profession. Maybe. But it is a profession, and as such, involves craft, even if it is practiced alone. I want this book to be there when you need advice on elements of craft, but also when you feel the need, as we all do, to step back and examine the fundamental nature of this story-telling impulse that we are compelled to practice.

Fiction as Drama

PART ONE

1

Writing as Performance

RECENTLY, I attended a New York publishing party at which the subject of creative writing classes was the focus of a lively debate. My host was a well-established biographer who was helping a mutual friend launch an anthology of short stories. He had assembled for the celebration a handsome collection of writers, book reviewers, and several Ivy League literature professors.

It was one of those bright Indian Summer weekends when Manhattan looks like a movie set. The garden of the East Side brownstone was pleasantly lit by hurricane lanterns, and the caterer had provided smiling young people to crunch around the gravel walks, bearing trays of liquor and rich hors d'oeuvres. I, for one, was feeling quite privileged to be there.

At some point, when gin was still being served and the hot buffet table had not yet been laid, I sidled into a stand-up conversation concerning another friend, Marianne. She was a novelist, who had, according to the speaker, just accepted "internal exile" in the midwest, where she had taken a post teaching creative writing. Apparently, her latest book had failed to earn back its advance and had not been sold to the paperbacks. She was, it seemed, stuck in the ranks of "middle" authors, and fleeing New York would only worsen her plight. The murmured consensus among the five members of this conclave was that Marianne had condemned herself to frustration and failure and had probably set her career back by several years.

"I really don't think you can *teach* writing," offered a rotund agent, himself neither a writer nor a teacher. "People have been trying for decades, and I've seen very little evidence of success."

Several well-groomed heads nodded above the clicking ice cubes.

"It's a real waste," added my host. "I know Marianne. She'll go bonkers out there, trying to explain what a metaphor is to the Future Farmers." He sipped scotch and lowered his voice to a confidential whisper. "And, when the word gets out that she's had to teach . . ."

Again, there was murmured agreement. The implication was obvious. In the minds of these people, at least, teaching creative writing was a disgrace, a quasi-profession, analogous, perhaps, to astrology. The practice was widespread, but patently bogus. Any writer who *had* to teach creative writing was making a public admission of professional failure. To paraphrase that shopworn adage, "Those who can't, teach."

I stared down at the smoldering butt of a lady's cigarillo, wedged in the gravel near her toe. Having consumed enough Beefeaters to overcome normal inhibitions, I decided to challenge this arrogance. "What about John Gardner?" I asked. "He certainly didn't *have* to teach up at Binghamton. He once told me that he loved it, that he couldn't really write if he weren't also teaching." Around me, five faces assumed expressions of annoyed defensiveness in the lantern flare. "Teaching creative writing certainly didn't hurt his career," I concluded, surprised at the vehemence of my tone.

A thin professor in an expensive blazer took up the challenge. "John Gardner was an exception." His voice was precise, didactic, accustomed to authoritative pronouncement. "The fact remains, however, that *most* writers can't teach, and few teachers can write at the professional level. For example . . ."

"Ray Carver," I blurted out, interrupting the professor's rhetoric. "Joyce Carol Oates . . ." My cheeks flushed with embarrassment. Examples of talented writers who were equally talented as writing teachers were not easy to produce. Finally, in frustration, I added, ". . . me. I teach writing and I write both fiction and nonfiction." Again, the gin overwhelmed caution. "And I do both damn well."

Silence. A throat was cleared with theatrical clarity. The professor presented me with his smooth, blue shoulder. The blatancy of my gaffe was suddenly apparent. I was, to them, just as much a "middle" author as Marianne. Everything I tried to say in our mutual defense only strengthened their prejudice. My host signalled a suntanned waitress to bring fresh drinks. I stepped back from the group. As I did, they resumed the conversation. Clearly, I had not stated my case very well, but equally, they were not very receptive to my argument.

Making my way along the dim path toward the bar, I was tempted simply to dismiss them as provincial New York snobs who were badly out of phase with mainstream American writing. Yet I had to admit that I'd encountered similar attitudes elsewhere in the country, usually among English literature professors who often viewed non-Ph.D. writing teachers such as me with mixed condescension and curiosity. Like the New York *literati*, these academics clung to that perennial romantic myth that writing talent was innate, that the novelist's or poet's skills were immutable, an absolute, congenital quality. If a young person inherited such a skill, he would become a writer; if he did not, no amount of coaching, no number of writer's workshops or craft seminars, nevermind how well-intentioned or conducted, would succeed in teaching this intangible quality: talent.

I'd heard the argument at English Department cocktail parties from Upstate New York to El Paso, from Georgetown to Berkeley. Clearly, the view was spurious. Just as clearly, it was widely held, despite the ever-growing popularity of creative writing programs across the country. What most angered me about this mind-set was its hypocrisy. Nine times out of ten, the very people who scorned the teaching of writing as a pseudo-discipline accepted as an article of faith that one could teach the traditional performing and plastic arts: music, dance, drama, as well as painting and sculpture. Indeed, most of my academic colleagues believed that the *only* way a young person could achieve virtuosity in the performing arts was to undergo a rigorous apprenticeship, hopefully in a conservatory setting.

They were willing to believe that a student could be taught great skill at Julliard or the Bolshoi Academy, yet they refused to recognize that a similar apprenticeship could be applied to the teaching of fiction writing. In actual fact, these traditional academics, and their literary-establishment counterparts, failed to recognize the fundamental nature of imaginative writing: *performance.*

If I had learned one important aspect of my chosen profession over the years I'd been working as a writer, it was that the activity I practiced each day had a lot more in common with the work of the actor, the painter, the stand-up comedian or the opera singer than it did with philosophy, literary criticism or history. I had come to recognize that writing was a tangible craft, not a mysterious natural phenomenon that occurred in unpredictable spasms like tropical storms or earthquakes. Being able to write well was not a condition someone was born with or mysteriously acquired like epilepsy. People learned to perform well as writers, just as they learned to sing, dance and play the piano. Therefore, I knew, if writing were a performing craft that could be broken into its component elements and learned, the skill definitely could be taught.

Standing alone in the shadows with the watery remnant of my drink, I realized that I would probably never be able to win over those editors and critics. After all, they had a vested interest in maintaining the myth that the essence of the writer's talent was an intellectual mystery, an orphic gift, that was visited upon a select few. Then they, themselves, became a mystical priesthood who could interpret and, perhaps, mold the writer's unaccountable talent.

But I knew from years as a professional that writing was a practical process, a logical craft. Talented, successful writers were diligent, careful workers, not helpless puppets who were inexplicably tugged and jerked by the strings of inspiration. Genius was a pleasantly romantic concept, but it didn't pay the rent, or for that matter, the orthodontist's bill, or the Master-Card statement that swept in each month like a cyclical plague.

Early in my career, I learned that I could not wait for the mysterious forces of inspiration to overcome my intellectual inertia and move pen to paper or my fingers to the keyboard of my Royal portable. If I was going to survive as a professional writer, I was going to have to *perform* consistently, just like a violinist in the New York Philharmonic or a running back with the Denver Broncos. A successful television actress didn't wait for inspiration to overcome her habitual stagefright when she set about rehearsing for a new role; a sculptor with a commission for a bronze abstract in the lobby of a corporate headquarters did not pine away for lack of inspiring impulse before he opened the oxygen valve on his welding rig.

Professional performers, I learned, knew the elements of their craft intimately; they were in full command of their skills. When they practiced their professions, they marshalled those individual craft elements and applied them through a logical evolution of stages, of *rehearsals*, steadily improving—or at least trying to improve—from one rehearsal to the next. Almost always, they sought out and accepted the criticism of their peers. They moved from one stage of the rehearsal process to the next, actively seeking to improve the specific elements that combined to produce the skillful composite of their eventual presentation. By the time their audience saw the final performance, the rough corners had been rounded, the guy wires and struts of artifice had been left behind in the rehearsal studio. What they offered on the stage or movie set was the distillation of that long rehearsal process. And this process was often a group effort, a common struggle during which they were coached and cajoled, bullied and encouraged by their fellow professionals.

I was lucky to have discovered the often obscured commonality between writing and the performing arts during the first year I was struggling to learn my craft. It was a lesson I've never forgotten. The drafting process in writing fiction or imaginative nonfiction—from the initial selection of story concept, characters, and plot to note-taking, outlining, then on to the painstaking evolution from one draft to the next—was completely analogous to the performer's rehearsal process, from initial concept to opening night. Inherent in this process was technical skill, or, if you will, virtuosity. And, I came to realize, the quintessence of virtuosity was the ability of the performer (or writer) to recognize and fully control every element in his repertoire.

If a concert voice soloist, for example, has to produce a slow, sustained high C lament in a Schubert *Lieder,* she cannot be ignorant of the exact function of that musical element within the work. She must also be able to produce a good, consistent high C tone on demand; she has to know from long *rehearsal* how to form her lips, how to shape her throat and brace her thorax to sing that note. She cannot bumble onto the stage, close her eyes and simply hope for the best. She must perform as a professional.

Equally, I came to learn, a professional writer has to be in full command of the craft elements that make up his repertoire. He must understand, for example, how physical setting relates to plot action and character, how dialogue actually works on a *practical* level, not as a theoretical concept. He must be able to marshal original and evocative metaphor and imagery on a daily basis to shape the tone and mood of his work, just as the *Lieder* soloist uses musical tone consistently to mold the mood of her performance. And, once the writer has learned to recognize and consistently replicate the essential elements of his narrative craft, he then must become skillful at integrating these building blocks into the logical evolution of the drafting process—his lonely struggle in the rehearsal studio—selecting what is right, rejecting what is wrong for this book or that story, slowly, intelligently, from one draft to the next, using the criticism of his peers along the way, until "opening night," the final draft, the submission.

In my career, I was also lucky because I did not set out to make my living as a writer until I was thirty years old. I had seven years experience as a Foreign Service officer during which I slowly assimilated the theoretical concepts I'd been taught in high school and college creative writing classes. By the time I began to write full time, I had acquired enough maturity to accept the discipline necessary to undergo the apprenticeship leading to a career as a journeyman writer.

And that apprenticeship proved to be both long and difficult. During my first five years as a full time writer, I produced three novels and a clutch of short stories, but only my first novel, *Matata*, was published. Twenty publishers rejected my second novel, *Clinton is Assigned*, and I had to rewrite the book four times before I found a good publishing house to accept it. In the process, however, I learned a lot about my craft, and the book became a monthly leader paperback that sold over one hundred thousand copies and went into three translations. Five years into my career, I had begun to reach my professional stride and knew that I could expect to sell my work consistently if I carefully practiced my craft. Professionals, remember, are not paid to make mistakes. Beyond this professional security, however, I also began to receive a stream of favorable reviews, and, in 1975, I was awarded a professional writing fellowship from the National Endowment for the Arts—a tangible recognition that I had, at last, made the grade as an artistically accomplished writer.

To date, I've had nine novels and nonfiction books published by leading houses. Three of these books have been featured main selections of book clubs; three have done well as paperbacks. Two have been widely translated abroad, and the Reader's Digest Book Section condensation of my latest, *Into the Mouth of the Cat,* reached over fifty million American readers. I have also sold the motion picture rights to that book to a major production company. During this period I've had a score of articles and short stories published here and abroad. On the average, I've been writing and selling about one critically and commercially successful book every fourteen months for the past seven years.

That record might not seem overly impressive, but the effort coincided with my six assignments teaching creative writing at universities in the northeast, midwest and the sunbelt. Instead of proving a detriment to my productive career as a journeyman writer, I found that teaching the craft of writing actually made me focus more closely on my own craft and concentrate on improving my professional skills and work habits. This renewed dedication must have transferred to my work in the classroom as well, because I soon established myself as an indisputably successful teacher.

Most of my students responded favorably to the straightforward, practical approach I took to teaching. By concentrating on craft-formation and demanding that they master the self-discipline of the professional drafting process, I was able to instill in them a sense of pride and also the confidence that they actually had control over their work. They learned for the first time that *they* were in charge at every stage as they pushed a story or novel through the long, but logical, drafting process, from conception to research to outlining to rewrite after rewrite, until they had a finished product.

Obviously, not all of these students were sincerely interested in undertaking the disciplined apprenticeship of a writer. Many were too young to appreciate that this apprenticeship was not an instant key to commercial or critical success, but rather a shift in attitudes and habits that could be applied to the unavoidable drudgery of writing and lead to professional virtuosity.

But, for those who did embrace my methods, the results were dramatic. Adult students who had been writing for years were able to see their work published for the first time. Undergraduates won writing competitions and went on to sell their fiction. In the student evaluations of my classes, I consistently received the highest points in the category of practical benefits of the course. In short, the students in my classes were learning how to write fiction and narrative nonfiction at a professional level of competence. Several of my former writing students are now practicing their profession full time.

Given my record as a writer and as a teacher of writing, it's not difficult to see why I lost my patience with the august group in the garden of my friend's East Side brownstone.

But, at the end of the day, it was not because of literary snobs that I decided to write this book. The true impetus began five winters ago when I was completing a stint as visiting writer at the University of Texas-El Paso. The late John Gardner, who was one of America's foremost novelists and intellectually vigorous critics, spent a few days at the university during the annual literary awards week. We hit it off immediately, and ended up enjoying a couple of late nights across the Rio Grande in Ciudad Juarez, drinking tequilla and talking about writing. At some point the subject of teaching came up, and we exchanged ideas and a variety of carrot-and-stick techniques we'd developed to help students overcome their natural reluctance to expose their work to classroom criticism.

Gardner said he liked my ideas, and I was certainly impressed with his.

"You know," he added, "I've had a creative writing book in the works for years now . . . lecture notes, material I've worked up for the Bread Loaf Writers' Conference. Seems like I'm always too busy teaching or working on a new novel to sit down and finish it."

"I'm in the same boat," I admitted. "I've got a whole card-board box full of notes and syllabi, student drafts and rewrites, class-handout sheets on dialogue and imagery . . . you name it."

"We really ought to write those books, Malcolm," John said. "Writing isn't so different than farming," he continued, refer-ring to his childhood in western New York. "You till the ground, plant your seed, nurture the young plants and pray for good weather. . . . You sweat, you get up at night, worried about the crop. . . . A season passes, and, if you're damn lucky, you have a harvest." He frowned and brushed back his prematurely white hair. "But, you know, farmers can't just go on *taking* from the earth. They have to return some of what they've taken, to plow back some of their harvest as an investment for the fu-ture." He looked up and offered the boy's smile beneath his old man's eyes. "That's why teaching is so important to me, Mal-colm. We have to give back a little of what we've been given."

Nine months later, a few days before he was to have been married, John was killed in a motorcycle accident in the Penn-sylvania mountains. He did not live to see his writing book, *The Art of Fiction,* published.

I have dedicated this book to John Gardner. And I've taken his advice about making an investment in the next generation of writers.

2

The Dramatic Essence of
Successful Narrative

I N THE LATE 1960s, I left the Foreign Service and moved
to the Greek island of Rhodes to write full time. I soon
found that it was hard to explain to the villagers in
Lindos exactly what it was that I did each day when I sat
tapping at the typewriter up in the whitewashed tower of my
house. So, as my Greek became less halting, I eventually grap-
pled with describing the concept of fiction.

Unfortunately, my neighbors were not very sophisticated;
most of them had never read a book. They knew about Homer
and the *Iliad,* but few people in Lindos could have identified
the classical epics as fiction. To them, the heroic "old stories"
were compressed truth that had somehow come down to them
through the dark tunnel of the centuries. The Lindians did
understand journalism and contemporary works of history.
Greek society is one of the most politically active in Europe and
every party has its newspaper and weekly magazine. Histories
of modern Greece—each written from a different political perspective—abound.

So, one warm fall afternoon when I began to discuss my own
writing with Old Georgas the fisherman and Taki the donkey
driver, these villagers brought their own cultural viewpoint to
the discussion. As I stumbled through my clumsy dictionary-
Greek, they interrupted me.

"You are writing a book of history," Taki confidently proclaimed. "That is good. Greece is famous for its historians."

"No," I answered, "not history . . . a novel." But my slim *Greek Made Easy* did not contain the word 'novel' in its lexicon.

"You're writing poetry," prompted Yianni the barber.

"No," I replied in frustration. "A novel . . . like Katzanzakis, like *Zorba the Greek.*"

Apparently, they'd never heard of this famous Greek novelist or his work.

I tried again, keeping my well-thumbed phrase book handy. "What I am writing is like history. . . . It is, I hope, pretty, like poetry. But it is not *true,* do you understand?"

"Not true?" Old Georgas snorted. *"Ta Psemata,* do you mean you write *lies?"*

Wearily, at the end of my ready reserve of Greek phrases for the day, I nodded assent.

But they could not leave this tantalizing subject alone. Taki, ever the boldest of the donkey drivers, took up the challenge. "What you wrote in your book was not history and not poetry, *etsi?"*

"That's correct," I answered, hoping that they'd change the subject.

"What you wrote was not true?" Taki emphasized. "But you sent your book to New York and they sent you back a check . . . for many thousands of dollars."

In the village, there were few secrets. All the mail, for the foreigners and Greeks alike, was dumped on a common table each morning, and during the social hour of the daily mail-call the failures and triumphs of the local expatriate writers and artists became grist for the Lindos gossip mill. Naturally, they knew that I had received an advance check after selling my first novel.

"Yes," I answered, trying to choose the right phrase. "A business house in New York paid me for my book, for my novel."

"How much?" The standard, shameless village query.

"Five thousand dollars," I said.

Silent, respectful nods. In those days, such a figure was a fortune in Lindos.

"Bravo," Old Georgas croaked. "Bravo. You write lies, send them to New York, and they send you back a check for five thousand *dollaria.*" He clapped me on the back.

"Bravo," the others echoed. Firm, leathery hands reached out to grip mine. This display of respect was as guileless as it was explicable. In the ethos of modern Greece, a person who could actually sell a pig in a poke, who could, through shrewd business dealings and clever negotiation market a commodity for much higher than its true value, was the object of universal admiration. After all, Aristotle Onassis, the archetypical Greek magnate, had begun his own career, it was said, by selling a shipload of spoiled and condemned tobacco. What I had apparently done —sell a book full of lies to a gullible New York business for five thousand dollars—was just as admirably cunning.

"Bravo," Old Georgas echoed. "Bravo, Marco, bravo."

Over the years since that episode, I have often thought about the reality underlying my Greek friends' outburst of admiration. Is it not, in fact, amazing that a person can write a book that is not true—a story about people who never lived and never will, a series of fictional scenes that dramatize in vivid detail events that never occurred, in short, a book crammed with *lies*—and sell that book? And isn't it also strange that thousands of otherwise normal adults would pay a portion of their daily wages to own such a book of lies? In short, what value can there possibly be in fiction?

We all know that the characters in a novel or a short story, in a stage play or a movie, are fictional. But are their fictional lives, as Old Georgas the fisherman suggested, actually lies? A liar tells us about events that are not true, but does a fiction writer lie? I think that the answer to this last question is important. Every amateur writer should ask himself this question, for therein do we discover the essence of fiction: what I have come to call the dramatic core of narrative writing.

Consider for a moment these points.

An historian writes a book in which he states that the Mohawk Indians built a fleet of large sailing canoes, sent them down the Hudson River, and, in the year 1491, voyaged across the Atlantic Ocean to the Spanish port of Cadiz, thereby becoming the first Americans to discover Europe, and, in the process, upstaging Christopher Columbus. Is such a book fiction or an audacious lie?

The only valid way to answer the question is to read the book. If the text reads like a straightforward, standard history, but is stuffed with bogus data such as the names of the principal Indian mariners, the places where they built and tested their fleet, and the dates marking the major events of their voyage, then the book is simply an elaborate lie, what Georgas would call *ta psemata*.

But, on the other hand, if this book offers a vivid *dramatization* of the voyage, if the writer presents us with fully formed, believable Mohawk seafarers, if we are allowed to share with these people the excitement and hardships of the adventure, from the initial obsession of the expedition leader, Feather-on-the-Snow, to the stubborn resistance to the undertaking shown by the chief, Burning Tree, if the writer places us inside the perceptions, inside the very skin of young Bright Blanket that terrible gray morning in mid-Atlantic when Feather's long canoe is capsized by the blue whale, if the writer makes us feel the taut, dripping deer-hide line that burns through Bright Blanket's hands as the canoe sinks, and makes us smell the warm iodine musk of the whale's breath, and we see the shredded clump of sargasso weed on the foamy slope of the swell where Feather's boat has disappeared . . . and so forth, and so on. In short, if the writer uses all his fictional craft to breathe life into this improbable tale, then it becomes fiction, not an audacious lie.

So, you might ask, what's the difference? Both versions are patently untrue.

In my opinion, the difference should be both obvious and of vital importance to the serious writer.

In the pseudo-historical version of the tale, we are presented a series of bogus facts. We learn little or nothing about the lives, the personalities of the Mohawk mariners. The book is only a practical joke.

In the fully dramatized narrative, the fictional account, however, the writer employs all the elements of his craft to allow us to *share* the *human experience* of this adventure.

Once more for emphasis. History is a chronicle of events. But fiction is a shared human experience.

The methods the fiction writer employs to help the people in his story, his characters, share their lives with the reader, are the same techniques that the playwright (and the actor), the narrative poet and the folksinger, as well as the television and screen writer, use to dramatize their stories.

But still, the fundamental (although usually overlooked) question remains: Why should any of us *care* about fiction, dramatic, shared experience notwithstanding? We know that the actual events, the underlying story of the Mohawks' epic voyage never really happened.

The answer is deceptively simple: As we join with the fictional Mohawk sailors in overcoming the challenges of the voyage, we learn important lessons about fear, courage, faith and perseverance, lessons we can apply to the less dramatic voyage of our own lives.

Moreover, a writer soon learns that dramatic fiction is probably the only way he can share with the reader a character's thoughts and inner emotions. In other words, fiction allows us to reveal human feelings; history and philosophy deal only with fact and theory. Fiction has living, bleeding human characters, not lists of kings and progressions of logical symbols.

Fiction—the unquenchable human impulse to tell dramatic

stories—has been with our species for a long time, probably since *homo sapiens* first mastered abstract thought and the verbal skills needed to replicate that mysterious process. No, I'm wrong; storytelling, the dramatic compression of the important emotional events in our lives, undoubtedly predates articulate speech. Look at the graceful pastel bisons and the dappled mastadons on the sooty cave walls of the Pyrenées. In my opinion, the splendid cave paintings of our Pleistocene ancestors are a clear example of the human dramatic instinct. Those lunging hunters and fleeing herds are not literal *history*, a prosaic record of the day's hunt. Rather, they represent an attempt by the Cro-Magnon artist to distill, to dramatically compress the experiences of his clan or family.

The prehistoric artist and his audience knew full well that those lines of charcoal and russet chalk were not real bison and wild horses. But they also realized that they were not lies. Rather, they were a metaphoric rendering of true events, of true human experience. Our forebears, two hundred generations back in time, recognized that we could learn important lessons about our own emotional lives by creating drama.

Closer to the present, the archaic forebears of Old Georgas and Yianni the barber knew that the epic stanzas of the *Iliad* might not be historically accurate, but, when Homer described Achilles weeping over the broken body of his comrade, Patroclus, every Greek speaker from the Hellespont to Pilos also wept. There was truth, emotional reality in that poetic fiction. The ancient world was a dangerous, unpredictably violent place—almost, perhaps, as frightening as our own advanced civilization. Men knew about loyalty to comrades and death in battle from the fabric of their daily lives. Homer distilled, compressed and captured this reality and allowed his audience to share the lives of his characters.

Almost three thousand years later, the British writer, Henry Fielding, brought his audience another kind of drama, a prose narrative he called a "novel." Asked the purpose of this new form of story, Fielding replied, "To educate and entertain." In his answer we can find the essential fictional model to which our own writing should aspire. We fiction writers are not practical jokers, nor are we essayists, rhetoricians or historians. When Fielding stated that fiction should "educate," he meant that the reader should learn something about his own emotional make-up, his own humanity, from having shared the lives of the fictional characters. The entertainment component of his paradigm lies in the drama, the stage-acting, walking-talking-thinking-feeling nature of narrative fiction.

When he wrote *Tom Jones,* Fielding did not intend to produce a long essay or historical treatise on the British rural gentry; he intended to create real, three-dimensional people, humans whom the reader could come to know and who would act out their interesting lives. Fielding, we should remember, was a playwright before he became, with Defoe and Richardson, one of the co-inventors of the British Novel. Drama was an element Fielding understood intimately; he also understood an important secret about his audience: People were nosy, they were incorrigible eavesdroppers and snoops, they were obsessed with other people's lives. This obsessive curiosity could be quenched in dramatic narrative, just as actual stage drama had met this need for centuries. What Fielding discovered when he wrote *Joseph Andrews* and *Tom Jones,* was that drama could be made *portable;* you could put a novel in your pocket.

But like all good dramatists, Henry Fielding never forgot that plays were ultimately about the lives of *people,* perhaps set in, but not primarily about, history or politics or philosophy. As Lord Byron once said of Fielding, he was, "the prose Homer of human nature." More directly, the literary critic Edmund Gosse captured the essential genius of Fielding's pioneering work in prose fiction. "There is nothing unnatural or extravagant about the incidents which Fielding introduces," Gosse tells us. "But they are such as might be expected *inevitably* to happen to such very natural characters as the novelist depicts."

Ladies and gentlemen of the jury, I rest, as they say, my case. Fiction is a dramatic presentation of real people's lives.

There isn't much sense in trying to teach a creative writing class using Henry Fielding or Anton Chekhov or even Ray Carver for what my friends in the Ed Biz call an "instructional model," a teaching tool. From my experience, most unpublished writers trying to break into the big time with a *Mademoiselle* short story or a hardcover first novel, are intimidated by published, that is honest-to-God *printed*, fiction. A Chekhov story or Virginia Wolfe novel usually seems about as easy to reproduce as a World Series no-hitter to a Little League pitcher.

I am definitely not suggesting we all sit down and line-edit *Tom Jones* or *Ship of Fools*, then try to apply what we've learned directly to our own work. What I'm saying is that we should simply accept, once and for all, that effective, successful fiction has a dramatic core; that, like Henry Fielding, that old English guy with gout and a powdered wig, we fiction writers are essentially dramatists. We create characters who are actors; their stage is our setting, their speeches are our dialogue, the acts in the play are the scenes and chapters we write.

Now, having made this point, let me refer to my thesis in the preceding chapter in which I state that writing is essentially a performing art, a craft that requires a process of rehearsals that lead slowly from one practice session to the next until we have a polished performance. What you will rehearse as you move through the drafting process from character conception and through the drafts, is an essentially human drama. You will analyze each rehearsal or draft for strengths and weaknesses; you will apply your understanding of the separate elements of your dramatic-narrative craft—hopefully with objectivity—to your draft, and you will make adjustments and improvements, just as a director and the cast of a play or movie work their way through the unavoidable drudgery of the rehearsal process.

When you look closely at this process, you'll discover that the supposedly *separate* elements of your craft—physical setting, point of view, metaphor, dialogue, physical action, etc.—do not stay separate, one from the other, very long. The successful fiction writer, like the successful playwright-director, soon has his cast of characters walking and talking and emoting in various ways within a believable setting. The successful dramatist is able to meld, to *integrate*, the component elements of his craft, so that a character does not appear to be acting out a fictional drama at all, but rather sharing with the audience an important and fascinating period of his life.

Sounds logical, right? maybe it even sounds easy. Well, writing integrated fictional narrative is not truly hard, but you do have to keep your wits about you while you're at it. In that regard, I'd say writing is about as hard as sailing a boat or driving a car or, perhaps, flying a light airplane. It all looks very complicated at the onset, but, if you learn the basics and also how to focus your attention on the problem at hand, you'll soon see progress.

Now, having gotten the theoretical groundwork out of the way, let us proceed. Let's examine how the drafting process actually works.

3

Integrated Narrative
Technique

Melding Believable Human Characters into a
Dramatic Setting and Situation: the Fictional Scene

AS THAT brilliant writer, publisher, editor and teacher, William Sloane, once put it, "The keystone of all fiction is the scene."

I doubt that any serious professional writer would dispute this maxim. But my own experience teaching fiction workshops has shown me that, with few exceptions, the amateur writer rarely understands the true nature of the fictional scene, its components, and its purpose within the work, be it a short story or a novel. In fact, one of the turning points in any writer's apprenticeship occurs when he begins to think in terms of effective dramatic scenes, not themes or plot, or rhetorical statements.

Given the absolute structural primacy of the scene within fiction, I always begin my practical workshop instruction with analyses of my students' scenes. Their first assignment is to draft the opening scene of a story, a scene in which there are two or more characters who interact within a realistically rendered physical setting during a situation of actual or potential conflict.

I ask them to employ dialogue, physical action among the characters and to use some form of assigned point of view or controlled narrative voice through which relevant descriptive metaphor appears.

Normally, I hand out an assignment sheet on which I've listed these salient points:

Fictional Scene = Character
- Believable and Relevant Physical Setting
- Point of View
- Problem or Conflict Situation
- Dialogue (or Monologue or Thought)
- Relevant Physical Action
- Relevant, Original Descriptive Metaphor

Most students find this assignment an enjoyable challenge; they feel the professor is simply performing the obligatory basic-skills review at the beginning of the semester before he attacks the actual heart of the course. What they do not realize is that effective fiction writing—the subject matter of the course—is comprised of little more than those elements listed above, which, when skillfully combined or integrated, form an effective fictional scene. As they are about to learn, fiction is simply a series of scenes, one following the other. If a person can draft a scene, then analyze his work, identify the problems and strengths and proceed to re-draft—as many times as is required—until he has what I call effectively integrated fiction, he is well on his way to becoming a skilled professional writer.

I find, however, that many student writers balk when asked to follow through with this assignment, to re-draft the scene until they have melded the various elements into effective fiction. Rewriting is not as much fun as the original drafting. There seems to be a natural resistance among students to complete this vital side of the fiction-writing process. Normally I preach and plead, I beg, browbeat and cajole them when they display the usual resistance to mastering the drafting process. I go through my whole ritual about writing as a *performance;* I remind them that the drafting process is a series of rehearsals, that the writer—like the pianist or the actor—sets improvement goals from one rehearsal to the next. Some respond to this appeal; others continue to resist.

At that point, I switch to a higher calibre argument.

"Look," I say, "I am forty-five years old, and I'm a professional writer. I make my living by writing serious fiction, you understand?"

They do, indeed, understand. One of the reasons they are taking my course is that they want to learn the secrets of professional success. Fair enough.

"Fine," I continue. "Most of you are in your twenties. By the time you hit your stride as professional writers, I will be in my sixties. I'll be looking over my shoulder at the competition. What I'm offering you here is the chance to learn a fundamental set of skills and habits that will eventually allow you to write successfully on the professional level. What I'm really doing is cutting my own throat."

Usually, I pause here for dramatic impact.

"Do me a favor," I shout, suddenly all bluster. "Don't learn how to write. *Ignore* the drafting process. *Forget* the concept of the integrated fictional scene. I'm going to have enough competition from younger writers when I'm old without adding you people to the list. Do me a favor," I repeat, "just forget about the drafting process as rehearsal. Stick to your regular habits. Hope for the best. Who knows, maybe you'll get lucky."

This tack usually wins a few converts. Others find my approach amusing, but doubt that I'm serious. So be it. I wish them luck. Surely, they're going to need it.

For those who do accept the apprenticeship, however, this is what happens. First, they draft a fictional scene. Then they let me read it; next, we sit down and discuss the draft, prior to rewriting. The procedure works something like this:

A Contradiction of Terms
a draft scene by
Ruth Johnson

Warmth pouring in through towering rippled glass caused the walls of the small apartment to glow. Squares of light shone on the wooden floor, looking upward to curls of dust dancing in the sunlight. Stacks of textbooks and paper lay on the well polished desk, reflecting gold from their midst. Martha Phillips leaned against the sofa, reading. Her dress was folded over her knees, covering her with blue.

She heard the beat of heavy boots down the corridor. A brass knob pushed open the door, illuminating the thin figure of Helen Andersen, Martha's roommate. Martha eyed Helen's ivory skin through the splotchy make-up. She watched her sit down on the floor, coat twisted about her limp body, gaping about the room. She possessed a calm that Martha had never seen before.

"What are you looking for, Helen?"

"Nothing. I've just never seen it like this before."

"What do you mean?" Martha watched the snow drip from Helen's ragged blue jeans. She hadn't washed them in a long time.

"I mean, all this stuff I've been talking

about, it's all garbage. It's not really like
that at all. It's so plain, so simple." Martha
saw that grin break out on Helen's face; it was
wider than usual, and her eyes didn't tense up
like they used to. "It's like someone turned a
light on all around me," she continued.
"Martha, I see. I know God now. Jesus saved me."

"Yeah, I've been going to church for
seventeen years. It really gives you something
nice to think about." She smiled, straightening her dress.

"But you don't understand; I'm changed,
completely different. I'm not like I used to
be."

Martha saw the thin film of liquid spark-
ling over the surface of her eyes. "What happened?"

"You know Joe Waters? We were talking. All
of the sudden I could see. I understood that
Jesus died for me; He bore my sins. I'm clean. I
feel like a ten thousand pound weight has been
lifted from my shoulders. He set me free from
all that. That's what He did."

Martha caught Helen gazing directly into
her eyes. She turned away to look at her own
Bible, glistening in the sunlight.

"How did you meet Joe?"

"Standing in line at the Bursar's office.
He said that God told him to go there."

Martha's face lost its color. She shifted
her weight onto her other leg. "I find that hard
to believe. There's more to religion than just
hearing voices. He doesn't do anything for the

```
church anymore. I don't know what he does with
all his time." She felt Helen lean closer.
    "Martha, He's not the pink lemonade marsh-
mallow god everybody thinks He is. Don't you
see? He suffered for me, and I'm not gonna be
lukewarm." Martha saw the silly grin return to
her roommate's face.
    "I know that, Helen. I think it's really
neat. Let's go eat dinner."
```

When Ruth brought this draft scene to my office, I made several Xerox copies. Then I asked her to sit next to me at my long work table, rather than across the desk from me, so that we could both see the text at the same time. Next, I did something that surprised her. I asked that she read the draft scene *aloud*.

Like most students, Ruth was a little hesitant. "You want me to read the whole thing out loud?"

"It's drama," I answered. "Drama is meant to be heard."

She shook her head, uncertain, not defiant. "It's fiction," she insisted, "the first scene of a short story. People reading it aren't going to read *aloud* . . . not like a play."

Ruth was a nice girl, and potentially, at least, a talented writer. "Listen," I said, "trust me. If you have problems reading it aloud because of awkward phrasing, nobody else will read it, either silently or aloud."

"Okay," she said. "Here goes."

She winced as she read. We all do; it's like hearing our own recorded voice, or worse, like seeing ourselves on videotape. Pure, unmitigated embarrassment. How do actors ever do it?

They do it because they're professionals, that's how.

Ruth finished reading the scene aloud. "It's bad," she said, scooping up the pages. "Let me take it back to the dorm and do it again."

"Fine," I said. "What parts will you change?"

Already, she had the offending pages in her manila course folder. "Everything," she said, shaking her head. "I'll just do it all over again. So it's . . ."

She did not have articulate phrases to explain what she meant.

"*You* know what I mean," she added in desperation.

"*I* do," I said, "but I'm afraid you do not. You're going to sit down in your dorm and write another first draft. You're not going to analyze this one and correct the problems."

"But it's all so bad," Ruth insisted.

"No it isn't," I said. "It just does not work completely. Let's review the assignment."

She spread her folded assignment sheet before us on the table.

Fictional Scene = Character
> Believable and Relevant Physical Setting
> Point of View
> Problem or Conflict Situation
> Relevant Physical Action
> Relevant, Original Descriptive Metaphor

l right," I said, reaching for my yellow highlighter. "Let's see what you have done, and what you haven't done."

A Contradiction of Terms

a draft scene by Ruth Johnson

```
Warmth pouring in through towering rippled
glass caused the walls of the small apartment
to glow. Squares of light shone on the wooden
floor, looking upward to curls of dust dancing
in the sunlight. Stacks of textbooks and paper
lay on the well polished desk, reflecting gold
from their midst. Martha Phillips leaned
against the sofa, reading. Her dress was folded
over her knees, covering her with blue.
```

Awk sentenc patterr NO variet

Question: Where is POV established?

She heard the beat of heavy boots down the
corridor. A brass knob pushed open the door,
illuminating the thin figure of Helen Andersen, Martha's roommate. Martha eyed Helen's
ivory skin through the splotchy make-up. She
watched her sit down on the floor, coat twisted
about her limp body, gaping about the room. She
possessed a calm that Martha had never seen
before.

Awk, sentence pattern: did you read ALOUD?

cliché

Pronoun confusion: who is she?

"What are you looking for, Helen?"

"Nothing. I've just never seen it like this
before."

"What do you mean?" Martha watched the snow
drip from Helen's ragged blue jeans. She hadn't
washed them in a long time.

"I mean, all this stuff I've been talking
about, it's all garbage. It's not really like
that at all. It's so plain, so simple." Martha
saw that grin break out on Helen's face; it was
wider than usual, and her eyes didn't tense up
like they used to. "It's like someone turned a
light on all around me," she continued.
"Martha, I see. I know God now. Jesus saved me."

"Yeah, I've been going to church for seventeen years. It really gives you something nice
to think about." She smiled, straightening her
dress.

Question: Is this action relevant to M's mood?

"But you don't understand; I'm changed,
completely different. I'm not like I used to
be."

Martha saw the thin film of liquid spark-
ling over the surface of her eyes. "What happened?"

You need relevant action here to support dialogue

"You know Joe Waters? We were talking. All of the sudden I could see. I understood that Jesus died for me; He bore my sins. I'm clean. I feel like a ten thousand pound weight has been lifted from my shoulders. He set me free from all that. That's what He did."

Martha caught Helen gazing directly into her eyes. She turned away to look at her own Bible, glistening in the sunlight.

"How did you meet Joe?"

"Standing in line at the Bursar's office. He said that God told him to go there."

POV break: Who sees this? [scene does not build to dramatic pivot]

[Martha's face lost its color.] She shifted her weight onto her other leg. "I find that hard to believe. There's more to religion than just hearing voices. He doesn't do anything for the church anymore. I don't know what he does with all his time." She felt Helen lean closer.

gratuit "cigaret actior

"Martha, He's not the pink lemonade marshmallow god everybody thinks He is. Don't you see? He suffered for me, and I'm not gonna be lukewarm." Martha saw the [silly grin] return to her roommate's face.

trite

"I know that, Helen. I think it's really neat. Let's go eat dinner." > *Scene stops: it does not reach climax*

I began with Character. In her first draft, Ruth made a mistake common to amateur writers: she did not know who her most important character was; she had not chosen her protagonist, to use the proper term. Ruth thought that the scene was about events, not people. She felt that the incidents, the plot, was paramount, that what happened to her characters, the people in her scene, was more important than who they were. As I stress later, such misconception underlies the question I often hear in writing workshops. "What would you say is more important, character, plot or theme?"

Serious fiction, I always answer—the subject matter of this book—is always and only about the lives of people. Plot and theme are, in my opinion, irrelevant concepts. If they actually exist in serious fiction, they are simply convenient critical tools we can use when discussing the events and meaning of the characters' lives. In short, plot and theme have no existence independent of character.

Therefore, the first obligation when writing a scene is to reveal character, that is, to help your reader get to know the people in the story.

And you do this by allowing your characters to act out their scene.

However, it will help the reader discover who is the protagonist, the most important character, if you assign the powerful tool of Point of View (POV) to one character and one alone within a scene. Ruth knew this from earlier writing classes. But she did not fully exploit the vast potential of point of view, she did not *focus* this narrative perspective so that it became what I call the "Sensory Filter" through which the reader experiences the character's human experience.

Relevant setting was another potentially valuable element of the fictional scene that Ruth did not exploit at the professional level of competence. The tangible details of the apartment setting were merely *decorative* in the first draft. She did not employ them as stage props as would a successful dramatist.

Ruth also did not prepare a conflict situation; she didn't let the reader know much in advance about the differences and attitudes underlying the relationship of the roommates. There was no perceptible tension between them when Helen arrived to begin the interaction.

And so, as I went through the draft scene slowly with my yellow and blue highlighters, I discussed with Ruth the importance of each of the major elements of the fictional scene that I'd delineated on the assignment sheet and which she had tried to employ in her draft.

When we'd finished the critique, Ruth stacked the three pages of the scene that now looked like a kindergarten finger-painting class had been set loose on them.

"I'll have the rewrite tomorrow," she promised.

And this was the new draft Ruth turned in the next day.

A Contradiction of Terms
(Draft #2: Re-write)
A Scene by Ruth Johnson

Martha Phillips shifted her weight on the lumpy cushion of the old blue sofa and lay her Philosophy text aside on the small end table. She squinted. The winter sunlight pouring through the tall, leaded-glass window at the end of the small apartment was too bright. But she also found it very comforting. There'd been nothing but freezy rain and clouds since Semester Break, but now the sun had reappeared, and she could almost pretend it was spring. Wouldn't that be wonderful . . . the end of this semester, the end of four years of hard work . . . a summer of coaching the girl's swim team at Indian Sands, then back here again, but this time as a graduate student with a teaching fellowship. A real <u>adult</u> life, no more silly courses, no more dopey roommates like Helen.

Martha sighed, smoothing her hand on the well-polished oak of the end table. This last year had been impossible, not the courses, certainly, not the part-time job in the bookstore. It was Helen, having Helen Andersen as a roommate. Well, that was part of becoming an adult, finding out that first impressions could be so deceptive. She smoothed the blue wool of her skirt across her legs, then looked up at her desk. Text books neatly stacked, her course folders carefully lined up.

Across the narrow living room, Helen's desk stood like an obstacle, like a wrecked truck on a newly paved street. Overdue library books spilled over the end of the desk onto the floor. A jumble of loose papers took up one corner. The center of the desk was a heap of folders and text books, and the wooden writing leaf was extended like a sagging tongue under the weight of the piled "self-help' books. Martha smiled, then sighed again. All that junk the poor girl wasted her money on . . . Exercise to Inner Peace, You're Your Own Best Friend, The Happiness Diet. Martha laughed openly now; a week-old, half-eaten Twinkie sat crusty and almost mummified in the dry air next to the Happiness Diet paperback. Incredible, but certainly in character. Helen grabbed a hold of instant-nirvana fads as readily as she stuffed junk food into her mouth, smearing the latest disco lipstick layer in the process.

Martha reached back for her book, two more chapters, then brush her hair, put on her boots and off to the bookstore for the Wednesday night shift. She sat back, trying to find a more comfortable spot on this sofa. Below her, on the ground floor, she heard the outside door slam, followed by the clump of heavy ski boots. Helen; no one else made so much noise. And those stupid boots: an impulse purchase before Thanksgiving, as if a few weekends with the ski club would bring the poor girl what she wanted, friends, recognition, respect, and above all happiness. Only three more months, Martha reassured herself, as the clumping bootsteps climbed higher, just three more months and I'll be away from all this.

Cold air snuck around the tucked woolen folds of Martha's skirt. As usual, Helen had forgotten to secure the outside door after slamming it, and now, also as usual, she stood there with the hall door wide open, letting in the cold air. Couldn't she ever realize that somebody had to pay for the heat, that there really weren't any free rides in life.

"Close the door, please, Helen." Martha tried to keep her voice neutral, but she felt her fingers curling tight on the edges of her book.

Helen did not answer. She stood in the center of a sunny rectangle, threadbare booksack dangling from one hand, a sheath of papers

clutched up against her chest in the other. Her
pale skin was flushed, two perfect ovals of
color, as if she was a child who'd been at her
mother's rouge jar. But that was the only
evenly placed color on her face. The garish
lipstick and habitual eye shadow had been
smeared almost off. Martha could see the green
and crimson traces on Helen's wrist. Helen
gazed at the spider fern, hanging in its pot
near the window. She turned slowly, her vacant,
slack-jawed gaze taking in the bookcase,
Martha's desk, and finally settling on the pile
of paperbacks on her own desk.

"Martha," she said, almost whispering.
"Martha . . . it's all _new_ . . . look, can't you
see?" She pointed at the sunny square at her
feet. "It's all . . . well, it's all brand new.
It's wonderful."

Martha gazed at the end of Helen's extended
finger. The nail had been chewed down to a
bloody crescent. Below the finger, Martha saw
the ragged cuff of Helen's jeans. The jeans had
not been washed in a long time.

"I waxed the floor after my Psych class,"
Martha said coolly. "I figured you'd be too . . .
busy. You can take dishes an extra day. O.K.?"

Helen grinned stupidly at the floor.
"Dishes . . . ? She dropped her coat to the
floor. "No, Martha, you don't understand. I can
finally see it now. It's all new." She spun in a
slow circle, grinding street grit into the

polished wood beneath her cleated boots. "All
that stuff doesn't <u>matter</u> anymore. It's like
someone turned on this great big light." She
settled to the floor, to sit on her crumpled
coat. "Martha, I see now. I know God . . .
honest, I really do. All of a sudden I understand." She looked up, her eyes wide and
flickering. "Martha, Jesus saved me. He died on
the cross for <u>me.</u> Can't you see?"

Martha felt the warm blood rushing into her
ears and cheeks. Not again. She was sick and
tired of this. "Helen," she began, "Helen, darn
it, you promised, remember? No more pills, no
more dope. Ten days ago, you promised, you
put your hand on my Bible and you took an
oath. . . ."

Helen laughed. "Dope?" She giggled now.
"No, Martha, I don't need that stuff anymore.
I've got something much better."

In this second draft, we see that Ruth certainly did apply
herself to mastering the task of writing a fully integrated
fictional scene. Obviously, she had decided that Martha Phillips
was her protagonist, and that point of view was, indeed, a valuable narrative tool. Overall, she had made great strides of effectiveness in the second draft.

However, she erred in a way that many young writers do
when they set about to employ professional techniques in their
own work. Ruth went overboard, she tried to cram too much
into one scene.

In our second critique session, we discussed this point. And
Ruth agreed that she would let the draft cool off for a few days
—always a good move—then set about to tone down the ex-
cesses.

Here is the third draft of the scene that she turned in a week later. I think that you will agree that Ruth Johnson was on her way to acquiring the habits and skills of a professional writer.

A Contradiction of Terms
(Draft #3: Re-write)
A Scene by Ruth Johnson

Martha Phillips shifted her weight on the lumpy sofa and lay her philosophy text aside. She squinted. The winter afternoon sunlight scattering through the leaded-glass window at the end of the room was too bright. But she found the warmth comforting. There'd been nothing but freezy rain and clouds since Semester Break. Now the sun had reappeared, and she could almost pretend it was spring. She stretched beneath the blue wool of her skirt. Spring was almost summer. By next winter, she would be in grad school, an adult. No more silly courses, no more dopey roommates like Helen.

Martha sighed, smoothing her hand on the well-polished oak of the end table. This last year had been impossible, not the courses, certainly, not the job in the bookstore. It was Helen, having Helen Andersen as a roommate. She smoothed the blue wool of her skirt across her legs, then looked up at her desk. Thick, darkly bound books neatly stacked, her course folders carefully lined up.

Across the narrow living room, Helen's desk stood like an obstacle, like a wrecked truck on an empty street. Past-due library books spilled off the desk onto the floor. A jumble of papers took up one corner, and the wooden writing leaf was extended like a sagging tongue under the weight of the piled self-help books. Martha smiled, then sighed again. All that junk the poor girl wasted her money on . . . Exercise to Inner Peace, You're Your Own Best Friend, The Happiness Diet. Martha laughed openly now; a week-old, half-eaten Twinkie sat crusty, mummified in the dry air next to the Happiness Diet paperback. Helen grabbed a hold of fads as readily as she stuffed junk food into her mouth, smearing the latest disco lipstick layer in the process.

Martha reached back for her book, two more chapters, then brush her hair, put on her boots and off to the bookstore. Trying to find a more comfortable spot on this sofa, she heard the outside door slam below her, followed by the clump of heavy ski boots. Helen; no one else made so much noise. And those stupid boots: an impulse purchase before Thanksgiving, as if a few weekends with the ski club would bring her what she wanted, friends, recognition, respect, and above all acceptance.

Only three more months and I'll be gone.

Cold air snuck around the tucked woolen folds of Martha's skirt. As usual, Helen had forgotten to bolt the outside door after slamming it. Couldn't she ever realize that somebody had to pay for the heat?

"Close the door, please, Helen." Martha tried to keep her voice neutral, but she felt her fingers curling tight on the edges of her book.

Helen did not answer. She swayed in the center of a sunny rectangle, threadbare book-sack dangling from one hand, a sheath of papers clutched up against her chest in the other. Her pale skin was flushed, two perfect ovals of color, as if she was a child who'd been at her mother's rouge jar. But that was the only evenly placed color on her face. The garish lipstick had been smeared almost off. Martha could see the crimson traces on Helen's wrist. Helen gazed at the spider fern, hanging in its pot near the window. She turned slowly, her vacant gaze taking in the bookcase, Martha's desk, and finally settling on the pile of paperbacks on her own desk.

"Martha," she said, almost whispering. "Martha . . . it's all <u>new</u> . . . look, can't you see?" She pointed at the sunny square at her feet. "It's all . . . well, it's all brand new. It's wonderful."

Martha gazed at the end of Helen's extended finger. The nail had been chewed down to a bloody crescent. Below the finger, Martha saw the ragged cuff of Helen's jeans. The jeans had not been washed in a long time.

"I waxed the floor after Psych class," Martha said coolly. "I figured you'd be too . . . busy. You can take dishes an extra day. O.K.?"

Helen grinned stupidly at the floor.
"Dishes . . ." She dropped her coat. "No,
Martha, you don't understand. I can finally see
it now. It's all new." She spun in a slow circle, grinding street grit into the polished
wood beneath her boots. "All that stuff doesn't
matter anymore. It's like someone turned on
this great big light." She settled to sit on her
crumpled coat. "Martha, I see now. I know God .
. . Honest, I really do. All of a sudden I
understand." Her eyes were wide and
flickering. "Martha, Jesus saved me. He died on
the cross for me. Can't you see?"

Warm blood rushed to Martha's ears. Not again.
Not another damned Nirvana trip. "Helen,"
she began, "Helen, you promised, remember? No
more pills, no more dope. Ten days ago, you
promised, you put your hand on my Bible and you
took an oath. . . ."

Helen laughed. "Dope?" She giggled now.
"No, Martha, I don't need that stuff anymore.
I've got something much better."

In the next chapter, we will use these drafts to analyze in
greater detail the function and requirements of the elements
that make up the basic building block of fiction: the dramatic
scene.

4

The Function and Requirements
of Integrated Elements within
the Dramatic Narrative Scene

YOU WILL NOTICE from the chapter title that I am still harping on the word "dramatic." At the risk of becoming tiresome, I'm just trying to employ a little good pedagogy here by repeating key concepts. And, if you take nothing else from this book, I'd hope that you retain the message that fiction is prose drama.

Having emphasized this, let's recall that the fundamental building blocks of any drama—stage, television, cinema or prose fiction—are its component scenes. Understanding what makes up an effective scene is as important for the amateur writer as understanding color theory and perspective is for the beginning painter.

A few years ago, I was giving a talk at a creative writing teachers' convention in the midwest and one eager young man from a small town high school got up and asked the question that has become perennial on such occasions.

"What do you consider more important," he asked with obvious sincerity, "style or plot?"

I'd been asked this question, in one form or another, at almost every teachers' conference I had attended and had my reply ready.

"I'll answer your question if you can answer mine." I paused theatrically for effect. "Which tissue system of your body is the most important, the muscle or the bone?"

Silence in the bright, overheated auditorium. Then an anxious rustle of whispers. The young teacher was in a painful posture, not quite upright, but not yet committed to sit down. I realized that my answer had left him literally hanging in embarrassed isolation.

"Look," I said, smiling as benignly as I could, "everybody asks that question. It's obligatory at these meetings, so don't feel bad." The young man grinned and sank all the way to his seat. I smiled now at the whole audience and continued. "Style," I said, "is a critical concept. So is plot. Scholars and book reviewers, and, I suppose, even some normal readers, isolate style and plot from the organic body of the fictional story. But most readers don't think about these concepts when they're reading, and certainly most good writers I know do not, either."

A stout, severe, older woman rose on the left of the auditorium. I could see that my tack was upsetting her. "If we don't try to teach students about literary style," she asked in a surprisingly mild voice, "how will they have any models to emulate?"

I couldn't really argue with that. In fact, I did not dispute her logic. "Let me try to explain," I began. "I agree that students should eventually produce well-shaped style and engrossing plots, just as music students should produce good tone and rhythm and student painters end up with good color and form. But nobody, not me, not you, certainly not a beginning writer, can simply concentrate on the finished artifact—be it style or plot—close his eyes, grit his teeth and hope somehow to produce it. We are ignoring the basic elements, the fundamental building blocks of fiction and looking at the finished product." I was stumbling now, searching for a good analogy. "An architect has to understand brick laying. "I blurted out. The analogy seemed to register. "Anyone who builds anything must understand the material, the structural components of the medium.

Plot and style are the end result, not what we begin with."

"What do we begin with, then?" The man's voice was clear, animated, from somewhere near the back of the hall.

"Scene," I shot back. "We begin with scene, and scene begins with character. Good fiction is always a shared human experience, the life of a character. The writer dramatizes certain important events in fictional people's lives, and these events become scenes . . . and from these scenes we get a story, and in the story we can—at some later date, if we must—isolate such concepts as plot and style."

Now, in the stuffy, sunlit room, I had their attention and I began to unfurl my sermon about the primacy of dramatic scene.

The first thing I did was to scrawl my favorite diagram on the smudgy green chalk board.

Fiction Scene = Character (in)
- Believable and Relevant Physical Setting (Relevant Setting-Situation)
- Point of View (Sensory Filter) = Voice
- Dramatic Action = Physical Movement and Dialogue
- Conflict or Problem
- Descriptive Language = Relevant Metaphor

Once I'd laid out the basic elements of the fictional scene, I began by discussing exactly what I meant when I said fiction was a "shared human experience."

I think many writers lose sight of this important point. Fiction is not essay; it is not rhetoric, written to persuade the reader about the justice of some cause. Fiction appeals to the emotional levels of our minds, not directly to our logical intellect. Of course, there are hundreds of great political novels, and many have succeeded in persuading readers when political rhetoric has failed. There is also historical, scientific and religious fiction.

But, for me, what all effective fiction has in common—regardless of the themes arising in the story-lines—is that the reader eventually feels involved in the lives of the characters.

I've had students tell me that they want to write "about abortion" or "about the drug problem" or "about parent-child relationships." I always answer: "Whose abortion?" "Who has a drug problem?" "Which parents and which children?" Fiction, I repeatedly stress, is about people, not abstractions.

Jim Hall, a friend, and a successful poet and writing teacher, traditionally tells his poetry students never to write a poem about anything you can't put out in front of you on the table. A poem is about a set of car keys, a subway token, a ripped sweat sock, and, if you must, a dried corsage of violets. It is not about LOVE, DEATH, JUSTICE (and, of course, INJUSTICE). Those are abstractions dear to the hearts of sophomores all across the northern hemisphere of this planet. But they have no place in true poetry, as Jim correctly stresses.

Using Jim Hall's method, I tell my students never to write about any subject unless they can *see* the faces of their characters, unless they can feel the fictional "reality" that surrounds the living, sensing people of their story. Certainly abortion is a rich subject for fictional exploitation, but only if the writer can make the reader experience the effect of abortion on the lives of believable characters.

Let me say one thing here and now. I use the term "believable" characters to mean characters with whom the reader can share feelings, emotions. I do not mean to suggest that all the characters, settings and situations of fiction must be realistic, i.e. close replications of the recognizable contemporary world. You can write about sentient plasma machines, swirling about in the energetic vortex at the core of some distant galaxy; you can describe ghosts and goblins—even plucky little fellows with furry feet and call them Hobbits—or scaly critters called E. T.

if you want to. Reproducing mundane reality is not the primary task of believable fiction. That task is to make the reader feel emotion: the shared human experience. But how can a sentient plasma machine in the Tau Centuri feel human? you ask. I don't know. That's your problem, if you're going to employ such beings as characters. All I'm saying is that your readers are human, so they can only truly empathize with characters that *seem* to have human emotions, be they Hobbits or gleaming robots.

We now agree, I hope, that fiction is about people, and that the reader gets to know these people—the characters of your story—through a scene or series of scenes that are written in what we call "dramatic narrative."

Let's move on to the next element of the scene:

Believable and Relevant Physical setting
(Relevant Setting-Situation)

The setting is the physical location of the scene's dramatic action: it is the place (or places) where the characters act out their prose drama. Think of it as your stage, your movie set, the barroom in "Cheers," the Precinct bullpen in "Hill Street Blues."

Physical setting is one of the most overlooked elements in scene writing. The setting is not simply any old place you might happen to choose to reveal your drama. Setting has an organic relationship to character and action. Consider the draft scene in the previous chapter and ask yourself: What was the relationship between Martha Phillips, the fictional character, and the physical setting of the scene? Was this setting appropriate to the emotions the writer wanted the reader to experience with the character? Can you think of a better setting?

Now, expand your thoughts. Think not simply of the physical setting, but also of the character within that setting: try to grasp what I call the "Relevant Setting-Situation." By this I mean the place, plus the time of day, plus the people involved, and also the emotions of those people (or that single character). For example, the setting-situation of the draft scene we examined can be summarized as:

> Martha Phillips alone in her apartment, reading philosophy, late afternoon. Contemplative, serene, optimistically planning future. Only negative elements come from her roommate Helen's "side" of sunny living room.

When examined in this manner, the setting is never simply a place, but always a place that is peopled by a character in a certain emotional state. Where and when the action of the scene takes place has a direct bearing on who your characters are and what you want to dramatize about their lives. Taken one step further, we now see that certain setting-situations have greater or less potential than others. Example: showing Martha Phillips, sound asleep in the middle of her dark bedroom, does not have much potential, does it? She's asleep; she is by definition, unconscious. The only way the reader can share her emotional experience is by the device of entering her dreams, and that's simply a literary dodge for creating another kind of scene, because her dreams must happen somewhere in some dream locale. Hence, a setting-situation is needed in her dream world.

Now, the writer could have shown Martha working at the bookstore, or walking home from class, or in class, or in church, or in the shower, or talking on the phone in the lounge of the student union. But, ask yourself this: What dramatic potential do those setting-situations have compared to the one actually used?

What does the writer want to gain from this scene? What does any writer require? What is the purpose of this scene? What are, in fact, the requirements, the "potential" mentioned above?

Look at the next-to-last element of the "Fictional Scene" diagram. "Conflict or Problem." Somewhere in any scene there must be dramatically revealed some aspect of the overall conflict of the story. In this case, the problem revolves around the clashing personalities of the two young women, Martha and Helen. In order to dramatically render this personality rift the writer must provide certain information about the two characters. For instance, we have to learn that Martha Phillips is a mature, serious, intelligent, calm, religious student, in control of her life, who is optimistically anticipating a clearly delineated future. In contrast, Helen Andersen is a neurotic, compulsive adolescent faddist whose life is chronically chaotic.

There are several ways the writer could have revealed this information in this opening scene. An omnipotent, third-person narrator, the literary voice I call "the Loudspeaker," could have intervened in quasi-essay manner and simply stated that, "Martha Phillips was a college senior, a mature, serious, intelligent, calm, religious person, in control of her life . . . etc." And so forth for Helen Andersen. In this manner the requisite biographical data could be conveyed to the reader with minimal artifice. In short, we would have intellectually known who the two young women were, and we'd have understood why they were incompatible. But we would not have shared the human experience of their conflict; we would not have felt what they felt.

So, in my opinion, at least, the Loudspeaker narrative approach is not appropriate. It is better to choose a setting-situation with the potential to dramatically reveal the underlying conflict (with the required biographic character information) through assigned Point of View. I'll talk a lot more later about POV, the sensory filter through which the reader shares the character's feelings. For the moment, let's stick to the potential of the setting-situation.

First, we agree, I think, that certain minimum biographical data is necessary for the reader to understand the conflict. What is this minimum? Well, we need to know that the two women are university students, that Martha is serious, intelligent, calm . . . and so forth. And that Helen is a mess. Let's look at the methods the writer employed to dramatically reveal this.

In draft two we find Martha alone in the quiet, sunlit apartment living room. Notice that she is comfortable being alone, even though the lumpy cushion of the old blue sofa is not in itself physically comfortable. What does this dramatically reveal? Obviously, that Martha is a person with some inner resources. Also notice what she is doing as the scene opens. Quietly reading her philosophy text is what they call "in character." If Helen had been studying alone, she'd probably have Menudo or Boy George blaring in the background. Also notice that Martha smooths her hand across the well-polished table and the blue (a calm color) wool of her skirt. Now see how these serene actions (dramatic demonstration of emotional state) lead her to examine her desk.

This desk, like the philosophy text, the table, the skirt, and all the other items in the apartment the writer chooses, are *stage props.* They are relevant parts of the setting, not accidental artifacts, randomly distributed by the writer. They serve a purpose, and that is to convey information about the character. In short, the writer fully exploits the dramatic potential of this setting-situation. She uses her stage props carefully to help dramatize who Martha is, what she is feeling and thinking (in that order, I should point out), and also what will be the underlying conflict of the story.

In my opinion, she does this very well. By the fourth paragraph of the second draft, we know a great deal about both characters, about the conflict between them, and we have been drawn through Point of View into the emotions of Martha, the main character, or protagonist of the story. This setting-situation clearly had adequate potential for the writer to dramatically reveal considerable information. In other words, it was *relevant* to the scene as a whole.

Now, let's look at Point of View.

Like physical setting, POV is rarely well understood or adequately exploited by amateur writers. I always try to explain POV by first pointing out that we humans have in fact four senses other than "view"—sight. I sometimes ask my classes to write a closely focused POV scene with blind characters in order to demonstrate that what we call Point of View is actually a device we use to lead the reader into the character's feelings through all the character's senses: sight, hearing, touch, taste, smell. I indicate that we don't need POV in true drama because actors show the audience their feelings by dramatic craft: facial expression, posture, movement, gesture, and all the rest. Our actors, the characters in our scenes, can also employ such stage craft, but POV gives fictional characters an additional opportunity to bring the reader into the story.

Look at the way the writer employs POV in our rewritten scene. In the first draft, we don't get any sensory details directly connected to the character until paragraph two: "She heard the beat of heavy boots down the corridor." But in the re-write, we find sensory details focused on Martha right in the first sentence, "Martha Phillips shifted her weight on the lumpy cushion of the old blue sofa and lay her philosophy text aside on the small end table." We are thus feeling the setting through the sensory filter of the main character. Through her eyes we squint at the winter sun glare, and with her, we find it comforting. Catlike, we curled with Martha, beneath the smooth folds of the blue wool skirt. In only four sentences, the writer has snared us, dragged us in just where she wants us, beneath the skin, within the senses, of her protagonist.

Once we are there, we begin to actually share the feelings and thoughts of the character, her human experience. We are now closely bonded to Martha; when she lays aside her textbook and examines the room around her, we see it through her eyes, we touch it with her fingers, and so, we *react* with her to Helen's unpleasant entry.

I will talk more about POV later. Now I should examine the next basic element of the fictional scene.

Dramatic Action: Physical Movement and Dialogue.

I guess I'd better add the word "relevant" here because, as with all fictional craft under discussion, I'd like you to recognize the relevance of these elements to the eventual goal of bringing the characters' emotional life to your reader. In the case of the dramatic action of a scene, I've discovered that many amateur writers do not understand that there should always be a direct connection between what a character does, his movements, postures and gestures, and what he is feeling.

Let's take as granted that fictional characters are indeed analogous to actors. You, then, as writer, become both play-wright and director. You create the characters and you also move them around your stage (the setting) as you require. I, for one, certainly keep this analogy firmly in mind when I write. And I encourage my university writing students to visit rehear-sals of school drama productions, to sit in the back of the theater and quietly observe how the director coaches his actors to em-ploy this stance or gesture, that grimace or grin, throughout the long rehearsal process. Once amateur writers have seen a skilled theatrical director at work, they usually approach the problem of developing relevant dramatic action in their fictional scenes with a fresh perspective.

"Body language" is a concept that came into vogue in the 1960s when a lot of Aquarian pundits were re-inventing the wheel. Suddenly, we were all supposed to take notice of the way people sat in their chairs, and held their coffee cups, or the rigidity of their necks and elbows. The theory was that human beings—like the anthropoid apes—would always reveal their true emotional state through their postures and unconscious gestures, even while trying to mask these emotions by neutral facial expression. No doubt all this is true.

But dramatists understood this simple human trait thirty centuries before the idea became popular in Cambridge or Esalen. People unconsciously act out their feelings; we all know this. Little children instinctively recognize the angry posture of a parent, even if that parent is trying hard not to reveal anger through facial expression. When it comes right down to it, a dog or a cat is pretty astute at reading your body language. In short, gesture, stance, nervous fidgeting, and, of course, facial expression, are all basic human communication, methods people use to show others their feelings.

We now agree that the basic task of the fiction writer is to bring his reader into the emotions of his characters. So, the writer must consciously employ gestures, postures, movements, shrugs, grimaces, tics, knuckle crackings, scratches, nose pickings, belches, lip bitings, *et cetera,* to help his characters communicate their emotions to the reader.

For example, let's examine the first two sentences of the rewritten scene.

"Martha Phillips shifted her weight on the lumpy cushion of the old blue sofa and lay her philosophy text aside on the small end table. She squinted."

A less skilled fiction writer might have said instead, "Martha Phillips sat on the blue sofa, thoughtfully staring into space, unable to concentrate on her philosophy assignment."

Notice the difference. What we have, obviously, is the old "showing versus telling" problem central to all creative writing instruction. But, beyond that familiar issue, we see in our draft that the writer employs a *set* or sequence of relevant dramatic actions. Call it the one-two-three punch concept, if you want. Martha is distracted by the lumpy cushions, she shifts her weight, lays aside her book and squints. The way this set of actions actually works is: POV (feeling of lumpy cushion) triggers dramatic action (laying book aside) and leads to facial expression which mirrors emotions (squinting = contemplation).

You will see, I hope, that this sequence of actions was not arbitrary or gratuitous. She didn't scratch her ankle, stare out the window, bite a hangnail, then suddenly think, *No more dopey roommates like Helen.*

Beginning writers often will have their characters perform random, *separate* actions such as sitting or standing, removing or putting on garments, and, all too often, lighting or extinguishing cigarettes. This use of cigarettes as arbitrary stage props, totally irrelevant to the character's emotions, has lead me to label all gratuitous dramatic action or gesture "cigarette action." The character moves, but in moving reveals nothing about his feelings. This is gratuitous; the action has no purpose within the scene. We, the readers, learn nothing from it.

But examine our writer's choice of actions for Helen Andersen's dramatic entrance.

"Below her, on the ground floor, she heard the outside door slam, followed by the clump of heavy ski boots. Helen; no one else made so much noise."

These actions, which are heard through Martha's POV, but unseen by the reader, introduce a personality, not just a two-dimensional character. Helen is a blunderer; she stumbles blindly about her life. She is not controlled like Martha. Helen slams doors and clumps up stairs. That is who she is. Thus, her very first dramatic actions in the scene serve to introduce her personality.

Now consider: "Helen gazed at the spider fern, hanging in its pot near the window. She turned slowly, her vacant, slack-jawed gaze taking in the bookcase, Martha's desk, and finally settling on the pile of paperback books on her own desk."

There are some problems of cliché and trite expression here that I'll discuss further on, but, on the whole, the actions themselves are completely relevant to the character's emotional state. In the next paragraph, I'm especially fond of: "She spun in a slow circle, grinding street grit into the polished wood beneath her boots."

That one-two sequence of actions dramatizes so much about Helen's egocentricity and disregard for Martha's feeling, and also—through Martha's POV—about Martha's angry disdain for Helen's selfish faddism.

Also observe that the relevant dramatic actions make full use of setting details or stage props; in this case, Helen's heavy cleated ski boots, grit from the frozen sidewalks, and the polished wood floor on which Martha—the conscientious adult—has just spent considerable effort with wax and buffer. Here the writer is employing fully integrated craft. She has her characters acting out their lives within a believable and relevant setting, which is brought to the reader through the sensory filter of her protagonist's Point of View.

Now, let's move on to the next sub-component of the scene's basic elements: dialogue.

It's been said, of course, that articulate speech separates us from the other life forms on Earth. Maybe. But fictional dialogue should never be confused with the normal speech of *Homo sapiens.* The way we talk in the real world and the way characters speak in effective fiction have a number of key similarities and a number of equally important differences.

First, let's again ask ourselves about the purpose of dialogue in a fictional scene, that is: What are the functions and *requirements* of dialogue?

Like dramatic action and gesture, dialogue must be relevant to the character's personality and emotional state. And, like dramatic action, it must help the reader share the character's feelings. And, like recognizable actions such as laying aside a textbook or grinding grit into a waxed floor, dialogue must be carefully *selected,* not simply a replication of natural speech.

In the appendices at the end of the book, I clearly indicate what I think are the "Functions and Requirements of Effective Dramatic Action and Effective Dialogue." In this chapter, I'd like to concentrate on the requirements of dialogue within a fictional scene.

First, dialogue must sound believable; it must appear to be lifelike, natural, and also appropriate to the character who is speaking.

Thus, when Helen Andersen speaks, her flow of words is broken by ellipses (. . .). She doesn't easily finish her sentences. Her speech, in short, reflects her internal chaos. In contrast, when Martha talks, she employs direct, honest, declarative sentences. Therefore, we can agree that the writer has produced dialogue that is appropriate to her individual characters. They do not sound alike.

But what about sounding believable? Here, we're onto a very important point of craft. Dialogue should sound natural, but it should never attempt to actually replicate natural speech. In real life, much of our speech is meaningless social patter, a verbal positioning of the people involved that lays the psychological groundwork for the actual exchange of information. For example, most people in real life begin a conversation sequence with an exchange of salutations and polite queries and responses: "Hello, how are you? Fine, thanks, and you? Nasty (or nice) day, isn't it?" etc.

In fiction (or stage drama or film) there is no time to slavishly reproduce such natural speech. Therefore, remember: dialogue is always *compressed;* it does not duplicate all the social nicety of real speech.

Hence, in our rewritten scene, the writer wisely avoids all social salutation exchange. "Close the door, please, Helen." Followed by:

"Martha," she said, almost whispering. "Martha . . . it's all new . . . look, can't you see?"

Ask yourself, is this a realistic way for two roommates to start talking to each other? No, it is not. But, is it believable? Yes, it is. Why? Because we already know that Helen is weird, and that Martha is stern, even censorious. Thus the dialogue exchange is perfectly within the reader's character expectations for the people involved.

My point, obviously, does not simply apply to this scene. All fictional characters must avoid the gratuitous rambling of true human speech. The task of fiction is not to duplicate life, but to compress from the continuous flow of life's events the dramatic essence.

So, we exaggerate when our characters talk. Real people do not speak dialogue; they just talk. Effective characters never simply ramble on. Their dialogue is carefully honed and polished by the writer.

But still, the dialogue must sound realistic, not stagey. How do we manage this important requirement without resorting to slavish replication of natural speech? There are craft tricks, naturally. To begin with, listen to real people talking. Try to develop what critics call a good ear. You will notice that people use many more contractions in speech than they do in written communication, i.e., speech is much less formal than writing. And, you'll notice that people employ more informal idiom, cliché, and simple short-syllable generic nouns.

For example, a young man college student wants to ask a young woman student to dinner. "I would like you to join me for dinner at Chez François, the small new French restaurant that I have read about in the Style section of the *Post.*"

This is good, articulate English, clear and complete expression. But it is not human speech.

Reading such a piece of dialogue in isolation, of course, makes it seem even more artificial than it is. But, believe me, I often see similar stilted dialogue in the work of beginning fiction writers, and, I'm afraid, of many writers who have studied creative writing for years. For some damned reason, amateur writers think they have to make their characters sound like the fourteenth Earl of Essex. Although, even the Earl would never talk that way in real life.

Try this: "You know that new French place Jerry showed us in the *Post?* How'd you like to eat there tonight?"

Notice: "French place." People do not usually recall un-

simple dialogue

familiar proper names in speech. And: "How'd . . ." People do use contractions when they speak. And: "eat" not "join me for dinner." Use simple, generic nouns and verbs in dialogue. This, when combined with contractions, will give your dialogue a natural ring.

Finally, let's look at a very important requirement of dialogue that is often neglected by amateurs.

Dialogue must be a believable exchange of information between the characters involved.

By this I mean that dialogue must sound like a natural conversation, never like the narrator intruding to speak through his characters' mouths. For example, many beginning writers try to load their dialogue down with a great deal of biographical data, to use dialogue as a channel to explain their characters' backgrounds.

Ask yourself, is this exchange natural?

"Yes, Mary, we've been married ten-and-a-half years now. It's funny, thinking back how we met in college, and how your parents disliked me because I was poor, and because I wasn't even a citizen then. But now, I'm District Attorney, and your dad comes to me all the time for favors."

Certainly, such a blatant piece of narrator's intrusion has no place in effective fiction. Yet, I've had writing students show me dialogue that was every bit as clumsy, and, when I rejected it, they'd throw up their hands and say they couldn't think of any other way to get the requisite biographical information across.

Such loaded speech is what I call "Bob and Ray" dialogue. Those two comedians used to have hilarious routines in which Bob would portray a radio correspondent interviewing historical figures such as Napoleon or Julius Ceasar. The routines went something like:

"Yes, General Napoleon, who has just been defeated by the Duke of Wellington at Waterloo, and is fleeing with the remnant of his once-grand armies, pursued by the victorious allied forces across the length and breadth of Europe, a sad travesty of the conqueror who once held the entire Western world in his thrall, yet, despite these setbacks, retains the love and devotion of millions of Frenchmen, ironically, considering that you are, General, not French by birth, but a native of Corsica, that mountainous island in the Mediterranean . . . etc."

Bob and Ray dialogue.

Avoid it. The temptation to use dialogue as an easy conduit for background information will always be there. But remember, Mary knew full well how long she'd been married and where she'd met her husband and what his present position was. Your characters will rarely have the opportunity to reveal their complete biographies to other characters in dialogue.

Once more for emphasis: Dialogue must be a *believable* exchange of information between the characters involved.

You can say a great deal about a character's background in a few words. Look at the end of our draft scene. "Helen," she began. "Helen, you promised, remember? No more pills, no more dope. Ten days ago, you promised, you put your hand on my Bible and took an oath. . . ."

Now, that is a reiteration for the benefit of the reader, a capsule of important background information about events in the two characters' past. But it comes across as a believable exchange of information because the writer does not rely on dialogue as the sole means of delivering biographical facts, and because Martha's exasperation has mounted to a point where it is natural for her to lash out at Helen and rub her nose in her past weakness.

On to the next basic component of the fictional scene.

We have already touched on the element of "Conflict or Problem." But let me expand on this important concept.

As my friend and fellow writing teacher Will Knott succinctly said in his seminal textbook, *The Craft of Fiction,* beginning writers should remember that fiction is always about people in trouble. I take this one step further. Fiction is *never* about people with no problem or conflict in their lives. At first examination, this may seem perverse, that literature, one of the most respected art forms of Western civilization, is entirely devoted to the negative aspects of life. Be that as it may, the fact remains, that all effective drama, on the stage or in the pages of a fictional work, involves characters faced with one kind of problem or another. This central core of conflict, of course, does not necessarily mean that the writer must accentuate the negative side of life.

John Gardner pointed out in *On Moral Fiction* that problem solving, human victory over adversity, was central to the human storytelling impulse. The eventual victory of the indomitable human spirit over injustice, illness, calamity and misfortune is a perennial theme of world literature. In short, fiction is about people solving problems, or at least about people facing problems and learning something about their humanity in the process.

Now, I realize that this might seem a tall order if you are a nineteen-year-old sophomore—or a forty-one-year-old office manager for that matter—who has never seriously attempted to write fiction. Don't misunderstand me; I'm not suggesting that you have to write epochal novels about the *Ultimate Victory of Good over Evil*. What I am trying to indicate is that fiction focuses on the normal human conflicts in our lives. Fiction does not have to be a Wagnerian tragedy or an afternoon soap opera, but your characters must confront problems in their lives, which will almost always lead them to be changed for better or worse by their experience, often as the result of insight or self-illumination. I don't want to go overboard here and start pontificating about literary form. Just bear in mind that there must always be some element of conflict in your fiction.

Remember that the most boring story in the world would involve a beautiful, healthy, well-adjusted child of a completely happy home, who passes an untroubled childhood and becomes an attractive, healthy, well-adjusted adult who makes a complete success of life, then marries a beautiful, healthy, etc. spouse, and they proceed to have beautiful, healthy, etc. children. A nice life, if you can get it. But who wants to *read* about it?

So, we must have conflict or problems as a central theme in our fiction, and thus, as a key element in our fictional scenes.

Note the element of conflict in our draft scene produces the desired result: tension. In fact, I have yet another formula here.

Conflict=dramatic tension.

This is just another way of saying that, once the reader is made to feel the problem (conflict), he naturally wants to learn the eventual outcome. He becomes interested. This interest spurs the reader to continue reading. Without tension, the scene is flat.

It should not be surprising that one of the basic structural problems of amateur writing is that of flatness, of bland lack of tension. Characters walk and talk, but there is no central conflict to unify them. For years I've seen this flatness in student fiction. And, when I point out the missing conflict, the young writers reply that nobody ever told them fiction had to have conflict that produces dramatic tension. I ask them if they've ever heard the story of Little Red Ridinghood or Hansel and Gretel, or the other gory melodramas we traditionally scare our children with. Naturally, they have heard these tales. Next, I ask where the dramatic tension would be if, instead of Ridinghood facing the Big Bad Wolf, her adversary turned out to be a friendly, floppy old English sheepdog named Mopsy, who never bit, but only licked the little girl's face. No conflict, no tension, no story.

Look how the conflict begins almost immediately in our draft scene (third draft).

In the first paragraph Martha has a minor irritation, the lumpy cushion. This is certainly not a life-threatening hazard. But it is a small element of disharmony. So is the bright sunlight, which causes her to squint. These irritants lead to speculation. She reflects on the long winter, both its physical and its psychological toll. This causes her to dream of the future, to escape the unpleasant present, which, we learn by the end of the paragraph, centers on her repulsive roommate, Helen. In short, the conflict seems to organically reveal itself.

I submit that this is a very elegant piece of craft. There is a sequence of perceptions employed here; the lumpy cushion distracts Martha, who lays aside her book, and squints, then longs for the future to be free of . . . THE CONFLICT (i.e. her dopey roommate, Helen). All in one paragraph. Notice also in the third draft how the writer has shed the clumsy and unnecessary background baggage about a summer job at Indian Sands and the teaching fellowship. These have nothing to do with the conflict between Martha and Helen. They're dead wood, and the author rightly discarded them in the third draft. Like all good writers, she was learning to envision the central conflict of the story as the framework of the drama, just as the steel armature skeleton is to a finished sculpture. The writer starts with a character in a conflicting situation, and fleshes the story out on that basic structure.

I will talk more about developing and expanding dramatic conflict later in the book.

Now it's time to discuss the final component of the fictional scene:

Descriptive Language = Relevant Metaphor.

Once again, I have found over the years that many amateur writers misunderstand the function of metaphor in fiction, just as they misunderstand the role of setting, dramatic action and dialogue. Like these components of fiction, metaphor must be *relevant* to character. Metaphor is not simply a pretty decoration that is arbitrarily and gratuitously pasted onto the body of the fictional scene like a "Have a Good Day" smile-face decal on the refrigerator door. Metaphor has functions and require-ments, just like the other functional components.

To begin with, let's look at what metaphor is and what it is not.

The word "metaphor" comes to English from the Greek *metapherein*, "to carry over." In this case, the sense is to carry the nature or essence of one thing, being or concept and apply that nature to a different thing, being or concept. The blood-red dawn. Sweet revenge. A heated discussion. By its very nature, a metaphor must compare two or more dissimilar things. We can say, albeit in trite language, "a golden apple." But it would not be metaphoric to say, "an applish apple." Or, "a reflective mirror." Metaphor, therefore is never redundant; it compares in order to increase or intensify, not to produce tautology.

One mistake many student writers make is to believe meta-phor must always be pleasant, inoffensive, in a word, *pretty*. But, what about this metaphor written by a combat veteran to describe the sight of a decomposing body? "He peeled back the crusted poncho and exposed a rippling curd of pus." Not at all pretty. But, is it effective? I think so. Notice especially the paired image pattern, "peeled back the crusted poncho" and "curd of pus." That is food imagery to describe a literally nau-seating sight. The reader is sickened, and that is exactly the emotion the writer desired.

Sorry to hit you with something so gross, but I want you to remember that effective or relevant metaphor does not have to be soothing, pleasant or pretty. It must, however, carry emo-tional impact. That is the main function of metaphor within the fictional scene. It should strike the reader's emotions, convey a sense of mood, an extended feeling, perhaps joy, tenderness, fear, repulsion, anger, or pride. In other words, metaphor al-lows the reader to feel what the characters are feeling.

And, by corollary, without effective metaphor, the reader probably will not be able to share the characters' emotions. Fiction is a shared human experience, right? So, obviously, effective metaphor is vital to the emotional exchange.

I realize that the very term "metaphor" is problematic for many young writers; it seems alien literary jargon. And I did promise to avoid the arcane nomenclature of literary criticism when I began this book. But, metaphor is hardly exotic. Metaphor pervades our daily lives; we perceive the universe around us metaphorically, whether we recognize it or not.

"He awoke to the song of birds." Nothing weird about that, is there? Just a plain decorative sentence. But examine "the song of birds." "Bird song." What is a song? In reality, a song is a musical verbalization performed by people to convey emotional information to other people. You can sing all day long to your cat, and he won't understand a damned thing. The canary in the cage chirps and whistles and peeps, but he isn't truly singing. Yet we always think of the sound he makes as a song; we cannot help but think of the morning "chorus" of birds as a joyful, sweet serenade. That, I maintain, is a metaphoric perception. In reality, if we had some supercomputer that was able to miraculously translate the meaning of the larks' and sparrows' morning song, the message would read something like: "Stay away! Keep back, you other ones! This is my territory. I am a strong male bird and I will puncture your vulnerable eyes with my beak if you trespass."

Nice song. Yet we find the expression "bird song" a convenient, an economical way to perceive the territorial warning calls of birds. Likewise, we find it convenient to describe ice-covered roads as "glazed," willows as "weeping," tall buildings as "sky scrapers," and so on. Hard mud is "baked"; stern policemen are "hardboiled," *et cetera*. Metaphoric perception and language is so pervasive in our lives that most of us never consider its function. Even the "hardboiled" detective testified in court last week, according to the Washington *Post*, that "shots *rang* out," at approximately 6:24 A.M. Shots, in the real world do not ring; bells do.

I once asked a class the derivation of the word "lousy."

Several said that it meant bad or poor or unpleasant. The rest of the class was silent. Then, one young woman said that she thought the word came from "louse," and by extension meant an infestation of lice. She won the gold star that day.

And what I think the class began to recognize is that our language is so, pardon me, *sodden* with metaphor that we have lost sight of its value as a writing tool. Of course, such metaphors as "hardboiled," "lousy" and "glazed roads" are trite, aren't they? "Shots rang out" is an obvious cliché, and thus has lost its original emotional impact.

I wonder how many of you know the derivation of the word "cliché." I went all the way through college, including some pretty good creative writing courses, before I learned what the word really meant. It's French, of course, and it comes from the verb *clicher,* to make a metal printing plate or stereotype. These etched plates were used in publications before the days of reproducible photographs. If, for example, Queen Victoria were going to visit Paris, arriving on the royal train from Calais, *Le Monde* would commission a *"cliché"* of the Gare St. Lazare railway station, showing the glass-domed tracks, locomotives wreathed in steam and the Republican Guard drawn up in ranks on the *quai.*

Such a piece of art might cost a lot of money. Once Victoria's royal visit was over, the plate, or *cliché,* could be used again for the arrival of other dignitaries at other train stations. Hence, through reuse, the original image lost its unique impact, its true emotional meaning. Some VIP due in Paris tomorrow? Trot out *cliché* 227: the omnibus "royal arrival" plate.

So, now that you understand where the word came from, you can better understand why clichés are, by definition, irrelevant to your characters' emotions, incapable of enhancing the mood of your scene. When we hear clichés such as "She was as good as gold," or "He was a real heavy hitter," we don't *feel* anything about these people. When you see a visual cliché like Rudolph the Red Nosed Reindeer on a Christmas tree, do you still thrill with the plight of poor lost Santa on that "foggy Christmas eve" when the only one who could save him was the scorned and denigrated Rudolph?

Effective, original metaphor, however, does have emotional punch. Without it, our scenes would be flat, lifeless. In a later chapter, I expand on metaphor. For now, let's just remember that it is a basic element of the effective fictional scene. Look once more at the third draft of our model scene. The fifth paragraph: "Across the narrow living room, Helen's desk stood like an obstacle, like a wrecked truck on an empty street . . . the wooden writing leaf was extended like a sagging tongue under the weight of the piled self-help books . . . a week-old, half-eaten Twinkie sat crusty, mummified in the dry air. . . . "

First, observe that these metaphors are not clichés. They are original comparisons of dissimilar entities. A desk becomes a wrecked truck. Its writing leaf is a sagging tongue, and a thoughtlessly discarded Twinkie is transformed into a mummified travesty of the original plump confection.

Do these metaphors carry any emotional impact? Sure they do. A wrecked truck reverberates with danger, waste, probably injury; certainly it is a chaotic image: a utilitarian vehicle, disabled, its cargo strewn about. The sagging tongue image is one of illness, grotesque distortion. And the mummy image for the Twinkie conveys the feeling of terminal repulsion.

Now look at the function of these metaphors within the scene. They convey very effectively the way Martha *feels* about Helen without the writer having to resort to the clumsy device of narrator's intrusion. She could have used the Loudspeaker voice to proclaim: "Martha was repulsed by Helen's chaotic and wasteful behavior." That type of intrusion would have communicated the essential factual information, but not the emotional impact; the reader would not have shared the human experience of Martha's feelings.

So, by re-examining the five basic components of the fictional scene, as I outlined them for the creative writing teachers that Saturday afternoon in Indiana, we can see what craft we must apply to our basic draft scenes as we move them carefully from one version to the next. In the following chapter, I introduce the concept of the "Rewriting Checklist," a valuable tool that I have developed as an aid in the vital drafting process.

5

The Personal Fiction
Writing Checklist

THIS CHECKLIST is a personal tool. Probably no two writers' checklists will be the same. The value of the list lies not in its length or complexity, but in its ability to help the writer consider in a logical, dispassionate manner what elements of craft he must apply when moving a draft scene, or a series of scenes, or, perhaps, an entire draft novel manuscript, from one version to the next.

Notice, please, that I said "dispassionate manner." This term might well disturb the romantics among us, those amateur and professional writers who persist in maintaining the glorious myth that writing *talent* is an innate gift, and that the act of writing itself is an unfathomable, uncontrollable gush of creativity. Any attempt to place rules or limits on this inexplicable creative miracle, they dogmatically insist, kills the writer's spirit, chokes the flame of passion. Therefore, they maintain, coolly delineating craft components and establishing lists of dos and don'ts can only stifle a true writer's natural instincts.

To these critics I will simply say that writing fiction is a craft; by definition, it requires discipline, which, in turn, involves acquiring and practicing definite skills.

I have sat with disciplined professional writers like James

Crumley and Ted Morgan and calmly discussed specific craft problems like dialogue tone and transitions between scenes. And I've sat across the desks of well-established editors debating the emotional impact of a metaphor or the relative merits of two descriptive phrases.

Having said all this, let me add that I would never endorse craft methods aimed at producing homogeneous work. I am not at all suggesting that your eventual scenes, your stories and novels must blindly follow rigid production formulae, and end up with characters and storylines that are so many thinly disguised clones. What I *am* arguing is that all effective fiction has common fundamental elements or components. But these elements rarely combine uniformly, with equal emphasis in different writers' work. The tone and mood of most fiction is not identical, or, for that matter, even similar.

But, in my opinion, all effective fiction is built on varying combinations of basic dramatic elements. These components combine in scenes as I have suggested:

Fictional Scene = Character (in)
$$\left\{ \begin{array}{l} \text{Relevant Setting (with)} \\ \text{Point of View (voice)} \\ \text{Action and Dialogue} \\ \text{Conflict} \\ \text{Relevant Original Metaphor} \end{array} \right.$$

What we have in this diagram is the core of your basic "Fiction Writing Checklist." Even if you're still impatient with so unromantic a concept as a checklist, please bear with me while I try to explain how this tool can help you.

First, another brief digression. Most young writers initially balk at the discipline, i.e. drudgery, of the drafting process. When I explain that carefully moving a scene or story from one draft to the next is the same as an actor taking his character from one rehearsal to the next, many students shrug and say that it's difficult to remember all the rules, and, more importantly, that trying too hard to remember these rules produces anxiety, and so they clutch up, freeze, and soon lose interest in the piece.

Certainly, that is not what I intended. I hope my methods will make writing well easier, not harder. But I also understand that writing is not natural, undisciplined behavior, no more than pitching baseball or playing the violin. As in these activities, the writer must learn to apply critical attention to his performance as he practices. In order to throw a good sliding curve ball, a pitcher *has* to learn to hold the baseball in a certain manner. Why do you think pitchers hide the ball with their glove when they begin their wind-up? Because there is only *one* way to hold a curve ball, and they don't want to reveal their pitch to the batter.

All right, there are an infinite number of ways to hone and shape fiction, but—like pitching—they all involve a handful of basic craft elements. The sooner you learn to employ those elements, the better off you'll be. And using an aid like the checklist will help you to consistently employ and integrate basic fictional craft elements.

I'm afraid that most amateur writers almost exclusively begin by pondering plot, unpeopled events, rather than by daydreaming about fictional people, and letting their lives organically evolve into dramatic story. But, regardless of whether you start with characters or storyline, eventually you're going to have to commit your ideas to paper. Some of you will want to use outlines of varying length and complexity. Many others will prefer to sit down and hammer out a first draft. Still others will combine note-taking with informal outlines, which then spur them on to drafting unoutlined scenes.

Whatever method you use (and I will discuss these different approaches later), you will eventually find yourself with a draft. And here is where your personal rewriting checklist comes into its own.

Let's take our first draft scene, "A Contradiction in Terms," as a model on which to apply a sample rewriting checklist. When you read this first draft, you'll notice that certain of our basic dramatic elements are there, in one form or another, but also that others are missing. In short, this draft is incomplete. I like to tell young writers that their draft stories are really the raw material of their eventual polished work. I say this because a draft has substance; it exists in tangible form and can be scribbled on, Xeroxed, cut-and-pasted, run through a word processor, shortened, lengthened, in a word, a draft can be *redrafted*.

Ideas, your initial thoughts, on the other hand, are nebulous, intangible. Dreams and speculations about potential characters in possible stories are fun to tinker with, but they tend to squirt back down to the lower levels of our minds unless we solidify them in some kind of a first draft.

So, I think we can agree that your first draft scene is your true raw material, your sketch, your clay. In this case, we have "Contradiction," draft one, by Ruth Johnson. When she and I discussed this draft for the first time, Ruth did something most students do in similar situations. She wanted to start all over again and write another first draft. As I suggest in chapter three, that is a natural attitude for an amateur writer. Ruth's lack of self-confidence lead her to a feeling of hopelessness. This draft is no damned good at all. I'll have to start fresh.

Almost always, this approach is self-defeating because the writer learns little from blundering into a new draft and piling up the same bad craft in a new stack. So, let's see what Ruth did learn by adopting a different approach. First, she took her assignment sheet and used it to begin compiling her personal rewriting checklist, even though she didn't realize that she was doing this at the time.

Fictional Scene = Character
$\left\{\begin{array}{l}\text{Believable and Relevant Physical Setting} \\ \text{Point of View} \\ \text{Problem or Conflict Situation} \\ \text{Relevant Physical Action} \\ \text{Relevant, Original Descriptive Metaphor}\end{array}\right.$

Ruth added this series of questions to the sheet as we spoke:

How does my setting relate to character? Are details used as props?
What is the dramatic potential of this setting?
Who is my main character (protagonist)?
What is her emotional state?
When and Where is POV established?
Is POV focused on Protagonist? Is POV reinforced?
Is POV consistent, or is it "broken"?
When does the element of Conflict first appear?
Does physical action (dialogue, expression, gesture, etc.) relevantly connect to characters' emotional states?
Any gratuitous "cigarette" action?
Is dialogue supported by relevant action?
Is there any line of tension developed?
Are there clichés and trite metaphors?
How can I add relevant metaphor?

By the time Ruth packed her papers away in her book bag, she bore an expression of confident involvement. I could see that she meant it when she said, "I'll have the rewrite tomorrow." Young writers often respond with such enthusiasm when they realize for the first time that they have absolute control over their own work, that they can constructively adjust and tinker with a draft to their own satisfaction, and that they now have a clear set of basic craft principles to follow as they work. They know that they are no longer *powerless* in the face of a mysterious process.

When she turned in her rewritten draft the next afternoon, it was clear that Ruth had made real strides toward mastering the skills of integrated narrative technique. By using her own informal rewriting checklist, she had succeeded in eliminating the major problems of her first draft and in building the new draft along much more effective and professional lines.

The first item on her preliminary checklist concerned the relevancy of her physical setting. As I immediately noticed in the new draft, Ruth had learned the basic craft procedure of using specific setting details as stage props to convey information about her characters' background and feelings. In this draft, Martha Phillips is introduced reading a philosophy text. When you consider this trick, you'll note its elegance. There's no need for a clumsy Loudspeaker narrator to announce that Martha's a college student. Who but undergrads read philosophy texts? Also, I was pleased with the lumpy cushion of the old blue sofa: your basic off-campus student housing. This sofa does double duty in relevance; it adds to character information and it helps establish POV. Obviously, Ruth had seriously considered the third question on her checklist: "What is the dramatic potential of the setting?"

As I read the first paragraph, I saw that she had erred on the excess side with her needless background information about Indian Sands and the future teaching fellowship. That was what I call telegraphing your punch, overdoing a good thing. She wanted to show Martha as serious and mature, but there were more professional ways to do it. I made a note to ask Ruth to add another item to her checklist.

Still in the first paragraph, I saw that Ruth had, indeed, considered the relationship of Point of View, protagonist identification, and mood. She established POV in the first two sentences with the feel of the lumpy cushion and the brightness of the winter sunlight. The reader was now perceiving the story through the sensory filter of the protagonist. In other words, the reader's attention was focused just where it should be, on the feelings of the main character. This sensory filter allows the reader easily to slip in and out of the protagonist's thoughts without resorting to the clumsy device of indirect dialogue tags such as "she thought," or "Helen pondered," etc.

You'll notice here that direct thought, or internal monologue is written in the first-person, present tense, and that it follows the same functions and requirements of normal dialogue. It employs informal speech patterns such as contractions and slang, and avoids polysyllabic nouns and intricate phrasing. By establishing POV early, the writer can jump right into the character's thoughts and thus unveil the conflict in a natural manner. At the end of the first paragraph of Ruth's second draft, I realized that she was now writing in an integrated, disciplined manner. The dramatic components of her draft scene were now working in unison, reinforcing each other.

In paragraph two, however, I noticed that she was again telegraphing her punches, overtelling by piling on needless background information. For example, I asked her if the reader needed to know that Martha's job at the bookstore was "part-time." A college student normally takes part-time work, so this bit of biographic data is gratuitous, awkward. In its clumsiness, the reader perceives the intent of the author as Loudspeaker, and the artificiality of the fictional process shows through. This, of course, is to be avoided. As the saying goes, readers—like theater audiences—must suspend their disbelief.

Ruth added an item to her personal checklist: "Is all background information necessary?" Notice in the third draft, paragraph two, that Ruth has eliminated the reference to the "part-time" job, and that she has also cut the blatant editorial statement, "Well, that was part of becoming an adult, finding out that first impressions could be so deceptive." By examining her draft for unnecessary intrusions by the author-narrator, Ruth discovered this clumsy intervention.

Clearly, she was learning technique quickly.

After we'd gone over the second paragraph, I pointed out that Ruth had inadvertently repeated the verb "to smooth" twice: "smoothing her hand" and "She smoothed the blue wool."

"Look," I said, "writers do this all the time. Awkward word repetition is a constant problem. But there's an easy way to avoid it."

"There is?"

"Yep. Remember to read your draft out loud, *slowly.* Listen to the words. When you've got an awkward repeater, you'll be surprised how it'll jump out at you."

Ruth nodded gravely, but she forgot to make a note on her rewrite checklist. Hence, in draft three, she still had the awkward "smooth" repetition in paragraph two. By the fourth and final draft, however, Ruth's checklist—now a more formal working document—began with the line: "READ ALL DRAFTS OUT LOUD FOR AWKWARD REPETITION!"

I later explained to her in greater detail something we all understand but rarely stop to consider. When we read our own writing, especially when its the second or third draft of a scene, we do not really register each word. Our eye automatically scans rapidly ahead. Thus we overlook awkward repetitions. But, if we read the same work *aloud,* we have to pronounce each word. The eye–ear–brain loop forces us to hear as well as see. We do, indeed, recognize when a word or phrase is inadvertently and awkwardly repeated. By Ruth's final draft of the scene, "She smoothed the blue wool . . . " had become, "She stroked the blue wool. . . . "

Before I left paragraph two, I asked Ruth if there was any more vivid or detailed way to describe the "textbooks neatly stacked . . . ?"

Why, she asked, wouldn't Martha have textbooks on her desk?

Sure she would, I answered, but why use a generic setting detail when you can reinforce POV with a specifically rendered and relevant stage prop? Thus is draft three, "Thick, darkly bound books neatly stacked, her course folders carefully lined up." This specific stage prop now provides a mood of mature seriousness, even of sternness—notice the ponderous emotional quality of the words, "thick, darkly bound." Isn't this an elegant contrast to the lightweight, silly books on Helen's desk? Ruth underlined the item, "Are details used as relevant props?" on her growing checklist.

In the third paragraph, I highlighted the verb "stood" in the sentence describing Helen's entry, "She stood in the center of a sunny rectangle. . . . "

'Stood,' I pointed out was a generic verb. It was without question the blandest, most neutral term we have in the English language to describe someone upright and stationary. Like most of these neutral, generic verbs such as sit, walk, talk, see, etc., the verb "to stand" had become a modern monosyllable from an Anglo-Saxon root. These are very old verbs in English, predating the enrichment of the language by the romance admixture of the Norman invasion. Such verbs are akin to the generic products now to be seen increasingly on supermarket shelves, no-name paper towel or green beans. They are utilitarian, but they lack emotional impact or flavor. As I pointed out to Ruth, we tend to automatically use the most common, neutral Anglo-Saxon verbs when we draft new material; they become a kind of shorthand. But such bland verbs rarely convey the emotional character information required in mature, well-integrated fiction.

By the third draft, Ruth had yet another item on her expanding checklist: "Check verbs for neutral generics, and add more active verbs when needed." You'll notice in draft three that the verb "She stood . . . " has been replaced by "She swayed in the center of the sunny rectangle. . . . "

I cautioned Ruth, however, about going overboard with fancy verbs; often the writer doesn't want to emotionally intensify an action. *That's* when he should use neutral Anglo-Saxon generic verbs.

Now let's look at the description of Helen's physical appearance. You'll see that Ruth keeps the POV tightly focused, so that the reader observes Helen through Martha's eyes. Notice especially, "The nail had been chewed down to a bloody crescent," and, "The jeans had not been washed in a long time." The metaphor bloody crescent was added to the second draft because Ruth had learned that she needed relevant metaphor. The echoing phrase, "The jeans had not been washed in a long time," is an excellent counterpoint. Here the sentence pattern is purposely repeated to echo the detached, censorious tone of "The finger. . . . " It's not "Her finger," but *"the* finger." Martha has begun to observe "the poor girl" as an object, not a person with whom she can empathize. And this important information is conveyed to the reader indirectly, through metaphor and POV reinforcement, not by the Loudspeaker.

Finally, observe how Helen's dramatic actions—"She dropped her coat to the floor," and "She spun in a slow circle . . . "—are perfectly relevant to Helen's personality and emotional state. Also notice how Martha has been subtly changed by the end of the scene. Remember that she was tranquil in the first paragraph, coolly contemplating her future. Now, warm blood rushes to her ears. She is thinking about Helen's "damned *Nirvana* trip." In short, she is angry. You will note how this POV reinforcement has eliminated the trite "She was sick and tired of this," Loudspeaker intrusion of draft two.

By the end of the third draft, Ruth Johnson had learned the value of her personal Fiction Rewriting Checklist. And this was how her checklist had grown by the time she finished her third draft of the scene.

Fictional Scene = Character
        Believable and Relevant Physical Setting
        Point of View
        Problem or Conflict Situation
        Relevant Physical Action
        Relevant, Original Descriptive Metaphor

Read all drafts out loud for awkward repetitions.

How does my setting relate to character? Are details
    used as props?

What is the dramatic potential of the setting?

Who is my main character (protagonist)?

What is her emotional state?

When and Where is POV established?

Is POV focused on Protagonist? Is POV reinforced?

Is POV consistent, or is it "broken"?

When does element of Conflict first appear?

Does physical action (dialogue, expression, gesture, etc.)
    relevantly connect to characters' emotional states?

Any gratuitous "cigarette" action?

Is dialogue supported by relevant action?

Is there any line of tension developed?

Are there clichés and trite metaphors?

How can I add relevant metaphor?

Is all background information necessary?

Are my verbs relevant and active?

Check verbs for neutral generics, and add more active
    verbs when needed.

Read draft aloud again.

Once Ruth had completed her third draft of the opening
scene of her short story, she was ready to proceed with the
subsequent scenes. And I was ready to work with her class on
the dramatic structure of their short stories, that is, where these
scenes were leading them.

This will be the subject of the next chapter.

6

The Dramatic Structure
of Fiction

RUTH'S CLASS seemed surprised when I asked them if they understood the function of scenes within a story. After some hesitation, one young man suggested that scenes were meant to "develop characters."

"Why bother?" I asked, playing the devil's advocate.

I was met by eighteen expressions of mild outrage. It was an article of faith, sacred to the collective bosom of all high school creative writing teachers that writers of fiction were obliged to "develop" characters. Now, here I was, the hot-shot Writer-in-Residence, who seemed to be questioning this basic tenet of the faith.

"Let me rephrase that," I added, trying to spur a discussion. "What, exactly do you mean by 'developing characters?' What is the ultimate purpose of this development?"

Again, I was greeted by troubled silence.

"Okay," I tried. "I'll put it this way. What happens to characters in fiction?"

None of the eighteen had a worthy answer. They were aspiring fiction writers, but they'd never been asked to consider the ultimate fates or functions of their characters. I quietly asked them to close their notebooks and suspend, if they could, their compulsive note-taking, to listen for a few moments to my version of what character development was all about.

First, I suggested, they should examine the fundamental model for all fiction: actual human experience. In our lives, events occur. We meet people; we have success and failure; we learn and forget. Every day shapes us in some subtle manner. We awake on any particular day in a certain state of memory, belief, expectation, anxiety, joy, anger or sadness (or combinations of all this emotion and knowledge), and, by the next day, we have been altered. In short, life inevitably *changes* us. No one can spend a week, or certainly, a month or a year without experiencing a change in the way he feels about himself, his family, and/or about the world.

So, if change is endemic to life, change must also be fundamental to life's dramatic mirror, fiction. Again, fiction is a shared human experience, and change of attitude, outlook and understanding is fundamental to most such experience in the real world. So, too, change must become fundamental as our fictional characters progress from the beginning to the end of a scene, through subsequent scenes, to the climax of a story or novel.

I'm afraid that my romantically minded colleagues might scowl again when they hear me proclaim yet another rigid rule or requirement, this one basic to the dramatic structure of fiction. But I would counter their outrage by asking for examples of effective fiction in which the principal characters either do not experience change or at least face the possibility of change or the possibility of acquiring self-knowledge. Characters may spurn this change or self-illumination, but all mature fiction that I can think of eventually leads to a dramatic moment at which the protagonist is altered in some way.

These changes do not have to be monumental; ideally, they are subtly drawn. For example, Martha Phillips has become actively angry by the end of the first scene of Ruth's story. At the conclusion of the story, she will physically attack her roommate, who—after a month's elapsed time—has embraced one more fanatical fad, the Hare Krishna cult. The most important change in Martha Phillips, however, is not the fact that she literally loses her cool and violently evicts Helen and her cult brethren from the apartment, but that Martha is shocked by the vehemence of her own rage, her utter lack of tolerance and liberal-Christian optimism. In the beginning of the story, Martha believed that a misguided "poor girl" like Helen could be guided and ultimately saved. At the end of the story, Martha's smug optimism has been shattered and she has been forced to recognize in herself a bleaker, more realistic and mature attitude.

In such dramatic fiction, the reader shares with the protagonist—through the effectively employed craft tools of POV, relevant setting, action/dialogue, and metaphor—the painful human experience of maturation. Martha was one way at the beginning of the story, and another way at the end. Change has occurred.

Once we understand that such change is a fundamental requirement of fiction (as it is with other dramatic forms), we can see that our stories should be written in such a manner that clearly leads the reader to the point of change (or rejected change, which amounts to the same thing). When I work with a class like Ruth's, I try to explain this by stating the obvious. Character "development" is actually character transformation or change. This development process usually has three stages. Simply put: the beginning, the middle and the end. We call these divisions of the story its dramatic structure.

When I was teaching in the midwest, I developed a reference sheet for my fiction writing classes, in which I tried to summarize fiction's dramatic structure. Although this typical structure is certainly not cast in bronze, the reference sheet does contain some valuable information for amateur writers. Often, students lack any clear notion of where their stories are going; as we have seen, they've been told *ad nauseum* that they must "develop" characters, but nobody ever bothered to enlighten them as to the purpose of this development. No one ever taught them that character change or illumination is the goal of fiction.

Let's say something about this structural format before we get into the reference sheet itself, however. Young writers should not slavishly attempt to duplicate the exact pattern suggested below. What I'm proposing here is a concept, not a blueprint. The dramatic structure of fiction—incorporating a Beginning, Middle, and climatic End—is an omnibus form, not an immutable paragon.

Here is a reproduction of an actual Dramatic Structure reference sheet that I wrote in the late 1970s. Let's see how the ideas have stood up over the intervening years.

> Mr. McConnell
> Reference Sheet #4
> English 405 T Th 1:20

Reference Sheet Number Four: the Function and
Requirements of Dramatic Structure in the Story:
The Beginning, the Middle, and the End.

  I. The structure of a typical short story or novel chapter is usually divided into three or more *scenes*. A scene can be said to be bounded by time, setting and action: often a short period of time, (a few minutes to a few hours), one setting (a room, a building, a small town, a car, etc.) and one major event (one dialogue exchange, one argument, one decision).

  II. Typical Story or Chapter Format: Function and Requirements:

    1. The Beginning:
      A. Establish relevant physical setting, using, when possible main character's point of view.
      B. Introduce, using focused point of view: the

major character or characters; their mood, background, age, profession, etc. (i.e., the minimum required biographical data.)

C. Introduce the conflict or "problem" of the story. This is best done through dramatic action (dialogue, etc.), rather than through intrusive "Loudspeaker" statement. Here, foreshadowing of later events is important.

2. The Middle (usually one or more scenes):
   A. Full development of conflict or problem; events foreshadowed in Beginning often come to pass.
   B. Characters introduced in Beginning often come together in setting foreshadowed in beginning. It is still possible to introduce new characters, if their appearance has been foreshadowed.

3. The End of the Story (Usually, one scene):
   A. The conflict or problem is somehow resolved; i.e., there is some intellectual or emotional *change* in the main character, or at least the chance for change. The character may learn some basic truth, and thus be changed. This moment can be called *The Pivot of Illumination.*
   B. No new important characters should be introduced in the End Scene(s), unless they have been foreshadowed. There should be no sudden, improbable shifts in setting. Beware the *deus ex machine.*
   C. Action, setting and narrative focus (point of view) combine to produce the Pivot of Illumination. Once this change has occurred, there should be no needless dragging out of any ele-

> ment, producing an anti-climax. Remember:
> don't try to say too much at the end; let the
> characters' actions and feelings speak for
> themselves.

You'll notice that this reference sheet contains my standard sermon: the primacy of POV, relevant setting and relevant action/dialogue. But there are a couple of new terms that I should explain, and also some exceptions that I must emphasize, so that you all won't charge off to your writing classes and say that stories or novel chapters absolutely must be structured in exactly this manner.

First, let me address the exceptions to this structural model. You'll see that I say "typical" short stories or novel chapters. By that term, I mean traditional narrative, and, by this term, I offer the great body of mainstream fiction that began in the eighteenth century and continues to this day. Such fiction encompasses the work of most serious writers, and many definitely unserious writers as well. We have in traditional fiction the work of Chekhov, Dickens, James, the young Joyce, Hemingway, Virginia Wolfe, and almost all prize-winning and critically acclaimed contemporary fiction writers. We also have within this rubric all the Gothic and trashy romance fiction that has recently captured so much of the commercial market in America. Most science fiction, both good and bad, can be found within this classification, so the dramatic structure I'm discussing clearly does not mean that your settings, characters and conflict situations must be exclusively realistic.

Once again, I am not proposing a perfect form that must be replicated. What I am suggesting is that *most* effective fiction incorporates these structural elements.

Usually, for example, we learn who the main characters are and are shown the basic setting of the dramatic action, as well as the primary conflict, in the beginning of a story (or in early novel chapters). All this does not have to occur—in that sequence—in the first scene or chapter. Fiction would be deadly predictable and boring if everybody always wrote this way. But, somewhere in the early pages of the piece, these elements will usually emerge.

The Middle of the dramatic structure is harder to define. For the moment, let's just use the cliché "the plot thickens" as a shorthand reminder that the conflict and its line of tension usually increase in complexity and intensity in this section of the drama. New characters still may appear, but their arrival usually is not totally unexpected.

The End of the drama almost always brings the resolution (or possibility of resolution) of the conflict. For example, Martha finally breaks with Helen. In the process, the protagonist often learns something about himself or about life.

Now, having said all this, let me quickly add that there is a lot of wonderful fiction that *seems* to break the "rules" of this structural model, and yet effectively offers shared human experiences. However, if we closely examine these seeming exceptions, we will notice that certain basic form is, in fact, observed: character, that is, protagonist, will always appear early in a work. The element of conflict, perhaps only nebulous disharmony, will also arise early on. Maybe a neutral narrator will prevail, initially keeping the reader distant from the characters' point of view, but, eventually, through one metaphoric method or another, the reader will come to feel what the protagonist experiences. And, ultimately, no matter how obliquely subtle the storyline, the characters will change or gain new knowledge, or at least be confronted with the possibility of such transformation, during which they learn about life.

So, amateur writers should consider my class reference sheet in the spirit that it was intended: an overly simplified guideline for students who have not seriously considered the structural elements of dramatic fiction.

Now, let me turn to the possibly unfamiliar concepts that appear in the reference sheet: Foreshadowing, *deus ex machina,* and the Pivot of Illumination.

Foreshadowing is a literary term that is also an important element of the fiction writing craft. My definition of foreshadowing is close to the dictionary entry: to indicate or suggest beforehand; prefigure; presage. In fiction, effective foreshadowing subtly suggests to the reader what he might expect later in the work. Please notice that I say "subtly suggests." Blatant or clumsy foreshadowing is a common sign of amateur writing. When the device is employed well, the reader is prepared in a generalized manner for later events.

For example, in "A Contradiction in Terms," Helen's religious ecstasy, as dramatized by her involuntary swaying and open-jawed expression, prepares the reader for her later transformation into a Hare Krishna cultist.

In the nineteenth century, helpful narrators would often intrude with such blatant foreshadowing as, "We shall see anon, dear reader, just how prophetic Percival's discovery was to be." We can't get away with this kind of intervention anymore, so we adopt less obvious means of foreshadowing.

If you are writing about a young person who is to experience his first sexual encounter, you might want to show him with an increased awareness of his own body. An eventual alcoholic collapse can be effectively foreshadowed by dramatizing a character's lack of self-control in an earlier scene. If a character is to die of a heart attack, show him experiencing physical malaise before the actual coronary event. In short, foreshadowing takes many forms and guises; it is a tool experienced writers carefully use to prepare the emotional ground for the major dramatic events of their fiction.

Deus ex machina is Latin, a term used to describe events in the conclusion of certain classical tragic dramas. Often in these plays, a god character such as Zeus or Apollo—the "deus"— would be physically lowered by a rope-and-boom—the "machina"—onto the stage to intervene in the human characters' lives, and thus, as they say, set things right and tie up all the loose ends. Classical audiences were accustomed to this device, but modern fiction readers reject it. So avoid introducing surprise characters at the end of a story, characters whose only role is intervention: a drunken truck driver who runs over your protagonist, just to conclude the plot. Remember, effective fiction is not about the action of the plot, but concerns the effects of these events on the characters. *Deus ex machina* characters who suddenly arise in the last scene are transparent plot devices. They have no role in the dramatic structure of good fiction.

Now I guess I'll have to justify the rather grandiose term "Pivot of Illumination" here. Eight or nine years ago, when I was more enamored with classy sounding literary nomenclature, I chose this expression to illustrate to my students the place in any fictional work where the character is confronted with the chance to change. Hence, the word "pivot."

One way I illustrated this concept was to ask my classes to consider the Book of Genesis. When the serpent tells Eve that she can eat the fruit of the tree of knowledge of Good and Evil, Eve is at the pivot point of change. She can resist, or she can give in to his blandishments. We all know what she did. Likewise, young Jim in Conrad's *Lord Jim*, up on the bridge of the ostensibly sinking *Patna*, with the other white officers down in the lifeboat screaming, "Jump! For God's sake, jump!" is clearly at a balance point of self-knowledge. He recognizes normal human fear in himself and leaps into the boat. He is changed, no longer the romantic proto-hero he thought himself to be.

These are just two examples of this pivot point in fiction. Every well-constructed story or novel that I've ever read has a similar point. Often the pivot does not involve clear choice for the character, but rather sudden revelation or insight. Throughout Joyce's *Dubliners*, the protagonists experience such flashes of understanding and are forever altered by their perceptions.

But, I see that I'm trotting out famous literary models here, something I promised to avoid. Let's look instead at more student work in two draft versions and see how one amateur writer learned to apply the dramatic-structure guidelines to the rewritten draft.

Bill Schmit
Eng 336B, Mr. McConnell

"With No Regrets"
Scene #1, First Draft

Dan Palmer lit the crumpled end of his cigarette and tossed the match to the floor of the rolling three-quarter ton truck. This was his last ride to the flightline, but Dan thought it was an unnecessary one. The Peace Treaty had been signed over three weeks ago, yet the 15th Aviation Company continued to fly its radio research mission over Quang Tri Province. Dan knew this was in direct violation of the terms of the Treaty, but he went along with it because home was getting closer and he didn't want any hassles that could prolong his stay in this filthy war.

It had been two years since he turned back near the middle of the International Bridge, just five minutes from Windsor, Ontario and a lifetime as an expatriate. It wasn't a decision he was ready to make. Going to Vietnam was like a death sentence, but if he could just outlast his twelve months there, everything would be all right, or so he hoped. Just don't kill anybody and you'll be fine, he thought.

But since arriving in Saigon's Tan Son Nhut
Airport that steamy, stinking morning last
May, he knew it was all wrong. Being there was
against everything he stood for. Lessons he
learned at the Waterford Baptist Church Bible
School kept coming back to him. Sitting in the
tiny room of the school, his neck chafed from
the starch his mother put in his collar, and
listening to the old wrinkled preacher paint a
lovely image of Christian soldiers made him gag
now in recollection. As the truck made its final turn and lurched sideways snapping Dan back
to the present, he found himself repeating
"Thou shalt not be in Vietnam." But now after
ten months here, he wasn't sure anymore. What
the hell did he stand for? This stint in the
Army had already cost him a girlfriend, his
father had died while he was assigned to radio
school, and now he was once again going to fly
and risk getting his ass blown away. For no
reason at all.

Dan looked across the truck at his best
friend, Mark Simons, sitting with his head in
his hands. The look of disgust on Mark's face
was all too familiar to Dan. He knew that they
both had compromised their beliefs by being
here. Dan looked for some comfort in the
thought that he wasn't alone in his feelings,
but couldn't find any. He watched as Mark un-
zipped the front of his Nomex flight shirt.
Even in February, this heat was unbearable. It
choked you with every breath and wasn't

something you got used to as time passed. Mark
looked up at Dan and said he wished he could
spend the rest of his life in an air-condi-
tioned bar. Dan laughed and said that if his
past was any indication, he was sure Mark would
get his wish.

"You know," Dan continued, "I wish there
was some way we could make this last flight
memorable. Some way we could screw the Army."

Dan had always felt satisfaction in
breaking regs. Wasn't he constantly being told
he needed a haircut or that his fatigues needed
pressing? Now seemed the perfect time to do one
last job for the war effort.

The truck jerked to a stop in front of the
Flight Operations hangar and they tossed out
their equipment and jumped to the hot PSP airstrip. Larry and Charlie, their pilots, were
already walking around the plane, a twin-
engine Beechcraft, doing their pre-flight
checks. Dan and Mark had some time to kill
before they had to board, so they walked to the
far perimeter of the airstrip, lit another
cigarette and leaned against the worn concrete
abutment. Looking out across the runway, a
smile came to Dan's face.

"Let's really screw 'em up down in Saigon.
Feed 'em some wrong information, some fake contact reports."

Mark moved closer to Dan.

"Sounds good, but how do we do it? They'd

never buy just getting the wrong radio messages."

    "No, but if we feed 'em a few incorrect
targets along with some legitimate radio messages, that'd give 'em fits wouldn't it?"

    "Dan, let's do it. It'll be our small con-
tribution to this war."

    They threw their cigarettes into the pile
of assorted beer cans and trash next to the abutment and walked back to the plane.

(Story continues . . .)

    What we find in this first-draft short story is typical of many inexperienced and untrained writers.

    I hope you noticed the flat "walk" and "look" generic verbs and the Bob and Ray dialogue. But they are not my main complaint. This concerns character motivation. Clearly, Bill, the author, told his story; that is, he completed the raw storyline or plot. In slightly over three manuscript pages, Bill showed us how Dan Palmer, an unwilling young Army flyer on his final mission, during the last months of America's involvement in Vietnam, conspired with his buddy, Mark Simons, to sabotage their combat intelligence operation. The two young men are part of an electronic surveillance plane's crew, and their mission is to pinpoint North Vietnamese Army units by eavesdropping on the "enemy's" radio transmissions. Both Dan and Mark hate the war and their country's murky, continued involvement three weeks after the official signing of the peace treaty. Their act of defiance is a small personal rebellion, of little impact on the broader strategic issues.

    That is the plot. Bill Schmit, like most beginning writers, thought that completing the plot was his basic responsibility.

But Bill did not realize what the plot—let's call it the dramatic structure of the story—actually requires.

He did introduce his characters in a more-or-less relevant setting, and he did raise the basic conflict. But there is no "Pivot of Illumination" of the scene. The characters experience no change or moment of insight. In short, the conflict does not lead to tension, which, in turn, leads to dramatic resolution. Examine this sequence:

```
     Dan and Mark had some time to kill before
they had to board, so they walked to the far
perimeter of the airstrip, lit another
cigarette and leaned against the worn concrete
abutment. Looking across the runway, a smile
came to Dan's face.
     "Let's really screw 'em up down in Saigon.
Feed 'em some wrong information, some fake
contact reports."
     Mark moved closer to Dan.
     "Sounds good, but how do we do it? They'd
never buy just getting the wrong radio
messages."
```

At this point in the plot, Dan Palmer undergoes a transformation from a passive malcontent to an active resister. Or at least he is supposed to be transformed. The way the first draft reads, he simply looks across the airstrip, smiles, and unveils his plan. There are no motives given, no believable reason for this rather dangerous act of rebellion. Certainly the reader is not allowed to feel what Dan was feeling, not permitted to experience the emotions of this transformation with him.

When I discussed this with Bill, he said that he would fully dramatize the pivot point in the next draft. Take a look at what he accomplished, once he understood that the dramatic structure of fiction required a Pivot of Illumination.

This second draft of scene two takes place aboard the plane after Dan and Mark have discussed sending in a few fake reports as a prank to punctuate their final mission in Vietnam. But what occurs to Dan in this scene is truly a pivotal point; it transforms him from a minor prankster to an actively defiant rebel.

"With No Regrets"
Scene #2, Second Draft

Dan was stowing gear in the back of the plane when Mark slammed shut the door. They crouched low to avoid the cabin roof, then climbed into their seats. They buckled themselves in and turned on their consoles. Dan stretched and rapped his knuckles on the low roof. The compartment was so cramped that he always got the feeling of being inside a garbage can. These planes were meant to carry six passengers, but since they had been converted to fly RDF missions, all the radios and electronic crap made it tight for two people, much less the three operators they were supposed to carry.

Besides, Dan and Mark could handle the job better without the third guy. Each one had his preference and never bothered to cross-train. Dan worked the scope, which looked like a small television. He would try to locate the radio transmitters from the signal Mark gave him. And Mark was happy operating the radio and taping North Vietnamese communications. While wait-

ing for final clearance to take off, Mark
punched the button on his console for the
private cabin intercom and called Dan.

"You all set? When a clear signal comes up,
I'll let you know. While I'm taping the real
thing, you shoot a friendly station near the
Monkey Mountain chopper base."

Dan keyed his mike and told Mark he'd be
ready.

"I'm glad we're gonna track some real targets along with the fake shit. Sort of mix
things up a little," Mark continued.

Dan was about to agree when he noticed a
white hospital plane parked across the taxi
strip. He got cold every time he saw that bird
with the big red cross on its tail. Bad news for
whoever was riding it. He watched as shiny
green body bags, obscenely bulging in the
middle or at the end, were being carried
aboard. The tags on the zippers were flipping
from side to side in the light breeze. Dan knew
it was those four guys from the 1st CAV that got
zapped last night by that 122 millimeter rock-
et. Why shouldn't the damn VC break the rules?
We were. Dan got pissed all over again. "Fuck
everybody. Four more grunts bought the farm.
Three weeks after it was all over . . . three
weeks!"

Dan got back on the intercom and pointed,
his finger shaking with anger, to the hospital
bird and the body bags. He shouted, "We're

```
gonna do it for them! Those poor dumb bastards
could've been us. All the fuckin' targets are
gonna be wrong!"
     Mark looked away from the vibrating window
and leaned back in his seat. He pushed up on his
helmet and wiped his right hand across his
sweaty moustache. His fingers stayed on his lip
while he nodded slightly, slowly.
```

In this rewritten scene, the Pivot of Illumination for Dan Palmer came when he gazed across the airstrip, and, instead of seeing nothing, noticed the large white hospital plane. The sight of the four bulging body bags with the remains of young G.I.s, just like himself, sends him into a spasm of rage. The peace treaty had been signed in Paris three weeks before, but still men were being killed. Now Dan had a *reason* for his active rebellion. He had been transformed, changed by what he saw across the hot runway. And he had clearly received an important insight: "Those poor dumb bastards could've been us."

I am not suggesting that the second draft of "With No Regrets" is completely integrated, faultlessly polished fiction. But I use these two draft scenes as examples of what can be accomplished once the beginning writer understands the requirements of dramatic structure in fiction.

Now that we have touched on the basic elements and structure of dramatic fiction, we can take a close look at the actual mechanics of the fiction-writing process from story conception to the conclusion of your final draft.

The Drafting Process

PART TWO

7

Practical Aspects of Storytelling

AS I MENTIONED in my introduction, the chapters in the second and third sections of this book will be somewhat less meaty than those in the first section. By now, you have been offered a solid theoretical foundation. You've learned the basic components of fictional scenes and the structural function of those scenes. The remainder of this book will serve, I hope, as a truly practical handbook to help you with the daily business of writing effective fiction.

In the Appendices, I've reproduced the various Function and Requirements reference sheets for your easy consultation, and there are several model Rewriting Checklists that you can consult when you choose to compose your own personal checklist.

Now I want to talk about notetaking and outlining. These are skills familiar to most writers, but rarely do writers follow the same pattern of habits as they prepare the first draft of a story or novel. For the purposes of this discussion, I will concentrate on preparation for drafting a short story, although the same discipline would apply to the preparation of a novel chapter.

First, let me offer an illustrative anecdote as to why I feel the formal discipline of notetaking and outlining is important for amateur writers (and professionals, for that matter).

In the late 1960s, I was a Foreign Service officer, serving in Tangier, Morocco. Tangier in those days was a cosmopolitan city with a well-established expatriate writers' colony, which included such notables as William Burroughs, Alec Waugh, and a variety of less-reknowned authors. Sanche de Gramont, the French-American novelist and Pulitzer laureate journalist was one of our neighbors. He and his poet wife, Nancy, became our good friends, and we often took trips with their family to the Riffi Berber mountain villages and *souks* near Tangier.

One such excursion was a weekend trip organized by the American painter, Brion Gysin, to Jajuka, a village in the southern foothills of the Rif. The people of Jajuka were professional musicians; they did not till the steep slopes of olive groves or graze livestock. All they did was play music—at local weddings, funerals, circumcisions and various healing and exorcism rituals —and they did it very well. They were organized into a guild that had changed little since the Arab conquest, eleven hundred years before. Their instruments were the resonant cowhide *tabla* drum and the piercing double-reed flute of Pan, the *raita*.

The village itself was spread across grassy terraces, halfway up a forested ridge. Olives and cypress separated the clusters of thatch and mud-brick *banco* houses. There were the usual chickens, dogs and cats, lots of children in tattered *djellabas,* and some braying donkeys. Our weekend at Jajuka was in April, a splendid season of wild orchids, poppies, lambs and kids, and, of course, the delicate silvery green of the olive groves.

The drummers and raita players entertained our group of ten *nasrani* foreigners all Friday night and well into Saturday with a hypnotically intricate set-piece concert that wound in processions through the torchlit village. By Saturday afternoon, I was near exhausted euphoria. We had brought wine and beer with us in our consulate pickup truck, and the men of Jajuka had provided potent Riffi *kif.* But it was not only the chemicals I'd imbibed that had so affected me. Only occasionally during my service in the Third World had I been so directly assaulted by the compelling music of massed and disciplined performers. The intricate rhythms and counterpoints of the night reverberated in my mind, melding with atavistic images of the goat-skin-clad *Boujaloud*—the ceremonial demigod of the festival—leaping through the flames of the campfire, his haunting pipe song echoing from the limestone cliff behind the village.

I knew that we had witnessed a performance of rare energy and beauty, a profoundly moving ceremony that few outsiders had ever experienced. And, I knew, that someday I would try to write about the experience. But, I also realized, it would be extremely difficult to capture anything approaching the truly magical essence of the previous evening. As I stretched out on the sunny grass for a nap, I saw Sanche de Gramont sitting with his back to a nearby olive tree, facing the valley below, and jotting industriously in a stenographer's pad.

I sipped from my icy bottle of PX Budweiser and called over to him.

"Hey, Sanche. What are you doing, writing postcards?"

Sanche focused his somber gaze on me and frowned with Gallic distaste. "I'm trying to take some notes about the music last night . . . about this *Boujaloud* figure. I think Brion's right, that the figure is pre-Islamic, maybe even. . . . "

"Yeah," I interrupted, moved now by the memory of the flaring torches and the echoes of the music. "That was one of the most incredible performances I've ever seen."

"Well," Sanche muttered, "I'm trying to take some notes, so that I can write a piece about it, maybe work it into a novel."

Now I frowned. Here we sat on one of the finest mountainsides in Morocco, in the weight of a rich *Maghrebi* sun, our bellies full of lamb and couscous and cabernet, and Sanche, ever the intellectual Frenchman, couldn't relax long enough to simply enjoy the world around him.

"Look," I began, unconsciously parroting the prevalent

counterculture ethos of the period, "you ought to just, I don't know . . . hang out, absorb this place naturally. You'll wreck the whole experience by trying to, well, *freeze* it in notes."

Sanche stiffened perceptively, then relaxed, his irritation tempered by thoughtfulness. "Malcolm," he said softly, "you get paid every month by the U.S. Government. Every month, whether you work hard or not. I get paid when I write books, and only when I write." I opened my mouth to protest, but his expression and tone silenced me. "You keep telling people how you're going to write one day. Well, in my experience, a writer is a person who writes, not just talks about it. You can usually tell the writer in any group. He's the guy taking notes."

I remained silent, my cheeks hot and taut, suitably chastised by his frankness. There was no arguing. Sanche was a professional writer, and I was a dilettante. A writer, he said, is a person who writes.

Later that afternoon, I trudged down the muddy trail to the valley, where we had parked our vehicles. From the glove compartment of the pickup, I removed the greasy pad we used as a mileage log, flipped back the used pages and made my first notetaking entry as an aspiring professional writer. Three years later, the descriptions of Jajuka that emerged from those notes became the setting of a chapter in the final draft of my second novel.

Earlier, I stated that your first draft is your true raw material. But notes and outlines of varying length and formality are also important resources. They are the tools you use to coalesce your swirling thoughts. I have found that notes and outlines serve to slow down my brain, so that I can seize useful concepts, characters, snatches of dialogue, and setting images from the chaotic procession careening through my mind when I am in the pre-drafting stage of a fiction project.

During this rather manic creative surge I am often tempted to sit down at the typewriter and just cut loose, to employ a method that I've come to call, "telling yourself the story on paper." Now, let me say here and now that there's nothing inherently wrong with this method. For some writers, drafting without the benefit of notes or outlines is the only way they can work. But I know that for me, and for many of my writing students, cold-turkey drafting—telling the story on the typewriter—is usually a very wasteful process. We tend to ramble and get lost in cul de sacs; chapters become mini-novels; scenes expand grotesquely until the reader is buried beneath a jumble of characters and events. The draft swells and clanks along to its ultimate conclusion, and we find ourselves with an interesting, but useless artifact. From the bloated draft, we must now cut entire sections, groups of characters, who, although of potential interest at some point in the draft, became irrelevant, once we understood the actual outcome of the story.

During the writing of my first two novels, I devoted—I almost wrote "wasted"—up to six months at a stretch drafting in this manner, telling myself the storyline of the book on the typewriter, going in fresh each morning, without a clue of the characters or events I was to dramatize that day. After a couple years of frustration, however, I learned that, for me at least, structured notetaking that leads to disciplined but not compulsive, outlining, was a skill I had to learn and practice.

The methods that I eventually developed have proven helpful to me and my writing students, so I've included them in this book. These are habits that I still use, and I know that several of my former students who have gone on to sell their work and to win literary competitions also employ these techniques. Here is a summary of my notetaking discipline as it has evolved over the past fifteen years.

Notetaking Methods

In order to take notes that will eventually help you write effective dramatic fiction, you must first have something to write on, some physical repository for the intangible burst of ideas and images that mushroom through your consciousness as you prepare a story. I have learned to always have with me some kind of notebook, and some writing implement. This may sound obvious, but many people neglect this discipline. If you're going to the beach, for instance, to lie in the sun, listen to a Brahms concert on your Walkman and relax, you might not necessarily pack a notebook and felt-tip pen with your blanket and sunglasses. But writers do. I have a variety of flip-open steno-type notebooks, some pocketsize, some the narrow, lined reporter's pads, some standard stenographers notebooks. I keep these notebooks available wherever I know I'll be during the day. When an idea occurs to me, I don't have to search for a paper napkin or an old envelope and something to write with.

At present, I have notebooks on my writing desk: legal-size yellow pads, steno pads, and lined three-by-five cards. In the living room, I keep a standard steno pad. There's a small lined notebook with sharp pencil stuck in the spiral spring binder on the dashboard of my car. On my bedside table, I keep a letter-size yellow pad and a penlight, so that I can congeal those shimmering flashes of insight that so often come to us on the banks of sleep, but which, inevitably, are impossible to recall in the morning. And in most of my jeans, walking shorts and suit-coat pockets, I keep a small lined spiral notebook.

For a while, I tried the device of dictating my notes into a pocket tape recorder. But I soon discovered that I had to transcribe these notations before they were of any use, and also, that I tended to lose focus and pertinence when I dictated. From this revelation, I learned that the actual process of taking a note, of putting pencil point to tablet or lined card, tended to compress and sharpen my thoughts. I made conscious decisions about my characters and the events in their fictional lives as I took notes. These rough, semi-legible jottings became important aspects of people's lives; I was writing biography, in a way, not fantasy.

Therefore, when the thought arrived that Joe Clinton's father was probably a railroad engineer, a crusty old Irishman who was both a drinking man and a womanizer, and a stern, moralistic taskmaster at home, I realized that this piece of background information would have serious implications for my protagonist. I had not understood until I made these notes *why* Joe Clinton was crippled by such a cynical, anti-authoritarian attitude until I jotted the background information about his father on my three-by-five card.

Joe's father never directly appears in the novel, only in the memory of his son. But Mr. Clinton senior's tastes, habits and world view definitely affected my main character. And it was not until I made that note that I began to grasp the connection between Joe's childhood ambivalence toward his father and his adult hostility.

I'm not suggesting that every note you jot will provide this kind of *petite Madeleine* flood of character insight, but I do believe that disciplined notetaking can serve to channel and mold the diffuse imaginative energy that engulfs a writer about to embark on a new work. When you take notes, you have to focus on your characters, and, for me at least, such attention spurs more insight into who the characters really are and what events are likely to occur in their lives. The seemingly mundane act of writing a note on a character's background or a setting's stage prop will force insight to emerge in your conscious mind.

A word here about the discipline aspect of notetaking. Ideas come to us at the oddest times. Often at dinner in a restaurant, a setting detail or a potential dialogue exchange will come popping to the surface of my mind. Carol, my wife, is completely accustomed to see me stop talking in midsentence and reach for my notebook. She understands that I am not being rude, just practicing my profession. She's a writer, too, and I accept her professional quirks. But other members of what they call polite society might not be so indulgent, especially toward young writers. One method I've developed to avoid embarrassment, yet maintain my notetaking discipline, is to frequently visit the toilet stalls of restaurant and bar restrooms. Public phone boothes work almost as well. At home, of course, or among close friends, I don't bother to use subterfuge; if they can't accept my notetaking, they aren't very close friends.

All right. We agree, I hope, that crystallizing your myriad creative thoughts in notes is important during the pre-drafting stage. But how do you organize the notes so that they will be of practical value when you actually sit down at the typewriter?

First, let me share with you an interesting discovery that is common to many writers. The actual process of notetaking in itself is often sufficient formal organization to shape your thoughts and feelings about the characters and the scenes of a story so that you find the notes themselves superfluous. In other words, once you've formalized your amorphous thoughts about a character or story, the components of the scene you're about to write are easily accessible in your conscious mind. You often discover that you do not have to refer very often to your notes, after you've gone to all the trouble to make them. In effect, the disciplined act of notetaking has replaced the undisciplined creative rampage of telling yourself the story on paper.

On other occasions, however, especially in long stories or novels, you will find yourself relying on your notes throughout the drafting process. Probably this dependence will be more pronounced in the early stages of your writing career than later. This being the case, it's important that you organize your notes in a manner in which they are of practical utility. Notes are no good to you if they aren't available when you need them.

Organizing Fiction Notes

I divide my notes into five categories:

> Setting and Props
> Character Biography
> Scene Action
> Dialogue
> Description/Metaphor

As with the other suggested craft tools in this book, these categories are not etched in stone. You may want to use a completely different grouping. The actual tag you put on a file, however, is of less importance than the notes themselves. Once I start to envision a setting, for example, more and more pertinent detail emerges. Just as Ruth Johnson began to *see* the titles of the self-help books on Helen's desk, you will be overwhelmed with relevant stage prop details once you focus your imagination on a rich potential setting. Events in a character's fictional background will burgeon, once you have begun to peel back the layer of years. When you start running dialogue exchanges through your mind, entire conversations will emerge. All this material is of great potential value, but only if you can snare it, pin it down on the pages of your notebooks.

As I indicated earlier, I make my notes on whatever pad or tablet is available at the time the idea occurs. Thus, by the end of a day, I might have twenty or more yellow sheets, torn steno pad pages, and file cards. What I try to do with this mess every evening is to carefully read each note, and, in the process expand on the original idea. I should emphasize that such additions are almost always a good idea. I usually read my note aloud, so that I'm sure I understand what I actually meant when I scrawled the message to myself.

As I employ a personal shorthand that's evolved over the years, I normally transcribe these cryptic phrases into standard English. If the note is of great importance, some fundamental revelation of character personality for instance, I sit down at my desk and type up the entry, expanding and emphasizing as I do so. Otherwise, I write out the note in careful longhand, so that it will be easily accessible when I start drafting. Then I staple the original note to the typed or handwritten transcription, and use a red felt pen and a yellow highlighter to point out the truly important information. I also use a series of personal symbols such as stars, circled asterisks and the like to alert me to key aspects of the expanded note.

Now I'm ready to file the material in its proper category. If,

for example, I have an important typed notation on my protagonist's biography—let's say Mario Conti's record as an Italian
Navy officer in World War II—I might go to the further trouble
of Xeroxing the note and its transcription and filing the two
copies separately, one in my "Character Biography" folder, the
other (marked "possible Flashback") in the "Scene Action" file.
In this way, I can be sure that I will make use of this important
information when I prepare my eventual outline.

I prefer legal-size file folders because my original notes are
often scrawled on a yellow legal pad before I transcribe my
shorthand. These file folders fit nicely into the cardboard portable file boxes they call the "Bankers Box," which are available
at any good office supply shop. By using these portable file
boxes, I can keep my expanded notes literally within my reach
as I sit at my typing desk. This way, I have my notes handy
without cluttering my desk, and I don't have to search through
the drawer of a filing cabinet to find a note and use it.

As you might expect, my five omnibus note categories often
lose their exclusivity as my notetaking progresses, but when I
feel a category doesn't quite suit the material on my page, I'll
Xerox the sheet and salt the copies through the working files in
my Bankers Box. By the way, I scrupulously keep these file
boxes separated by project. Notes for a short story do not strag-
gle into a novel file. Press clippings and background for a feature article are never mixed in with background for a screen-
play. I do accumulate a lot of files and Bankers Boxes, but that's
okay with me. These supplies are tax deductible, and the order
they bring to my work helps keep me organized.

I suppose some romantic souls might quibble that such habits stifle creativity. All I can offer in reply is my own record as
a professional writer. For the first five years of my career, I had
not yet learned these habits of disciplined craft, and I managed
to sell one novel. In the next ten years I followed the organizational habits described above and I wrote and sold eight books
and dozens of narrative feature articles, all to leading national

publishers and magazines. Success does not need apologists.

Before we leave the discussion of notetaking, let me expand slightly on the interesting connection between notetaking and imagination. Specifically, I'd like to mention how I work on potential Scene Action and Dialogue. Obviously, I consider fiction to be another form of drama; therefore my envisioning scenes and dialogue is analogous to a playwright blocking out the scenes of his play or film. In order to "test" a character's action or dialogue, I will literally act it out, not in my imagination, but physically, walking or crouching or crawling across the goatskin *flokati* on my studio floor.

By physically dramatizing what a character might undergo in a potential scene, I can learn the emotional surges and subtleties he will feel at important moments. Equally, by actually speaking dialogue, I can get the sound of it fixed in my mind. Then, as I take notes, the rhythms and cadence of the eventual dialogue exchange takes on a tangible reality for me. I have a strong sense of personal verisimilitude by the time I've completed my notetaking and am ready for the outline.

Outlines are a problem for writers and for writing teachers. Often in undergraduate university creative writing classes, the students never produce any work longer than a sketch or a short story of a few scenes. In work of this length, outlines are not usually very helpful. What I mean is that most of us approach the drafting of a one-scene story with the major characters, setting and events clearly conceived.

We imagine an encounter at an airport between two old lovers who happen to meet between planes. The setting and possible range of events and dialogue is easy enough to manage without a formal outline. We write a vignette about a teenage girl's first experience with bigotry. She's at her dance school and she accidentally overhears two respected teachers engaging in vicious racial slander. Again, the limited scope of locale and action does not require an outline. Such so-called "small" stories are often the practice ground for beginning writers, just as sketches help train most painters. But eventually, a beginning writer will want to expand to longer, more complex stories, and from them to novels. And, in mastering this expansion, he will do well to understand and use the joint tool of disciplined note-taking and structured outlining.

I am not suggesting, however, that all story or novel outlines have to be complex, polished constructions. And I want to stress here that elaborate outlining can often *interfere* with good writing by displacing the writer's imaginative energy; sometimes the outline becomes a sterile end in itself, a baroque surrogate for the intended story—ultimately, an excuse for not facing the unpleasant and risky challenge of the empty page. So, don't mistake my intention. I'm not asking you to outline your stories to death; I'm just offering an efficient and practical tool for you to use in coming to grips with your characters and their fictional lives.

Fiction Outlines

Outlines should not be dense, unwieldy documents. They must be easy to use, so they must also be brief. Never confuse a well-written outline with a finished story. And don't make your outline so watertight that there's no room for your characters to expand as you draft your scenes.

Having said this, let me show you a typical fiction outline of the type I call a "Scene List":

FICTION OUTLINE

SCENE #	SETTING / SITUATION	POV	ACTION / PURPOSE
1	Martha alone, off-campus apt. Studying before job, annoyed by Helen's mess, etc. *Stage props:* 2 girls' desks.	Martha's	Helen enters, spaced out on Jesus. Martha chides her about dope. *Purpose:* reveal personality-

SCENE #	SETTING / SITUATION	POV	ACTION / PURPOSE
			clash conflict and reveal both characters as opposites.
2	Christian Students Union, Campus Baptist Church (basement meeting room). One week later. Martha at Bible study class with other students. Dr. Reed, chaplain, leads discussion of Book of Revelation, very detached, scholarly—liberal *Stage props:* blackboard, maps, chairs.	Martha's	Helen bursts in with Joe Waters, born-again zealot. Challenges Dr. Reed's interpretation. *Purpose:* dramatize mounting anger and resentment of Martha, also her embarrassment.
3	Two weeks later. Outside apt-to-inside, night, last day of spring break. Martha arrives from bus station with suitcase, etc.—hoping for quiet remainder of semester. *Stage props:* drums, robes, wooden floor.	Martha's	Martha hears weird chanting, drums, etc. Climbs stairs to find Helen, head shaved, in saffron robe, with other Hare Krishna cultists. Martha explodes, violently evicts them all. *Purpose:* dramatize shocking unChristian anger inside Martha.

There are a number of interesting elements to this scene-list outline. First, notice that the concept of setting-situation is fundamental to the exercise. By using this format, the writer has to address the issue of the setting's dramatic potential (with possible stage props) and also the character's emotional state at the time the scene begins. By balancing the physical stage—the location of the scene's action—with the characters' states of mind, the writer can tinker and adjust his outline so that it provides the richest possible dramatic potential.

For example, Ruth could have chosen the living room of the Christian Students Union for the setting of scene two. But this relaxed domestic location does not offer the rich conflict potential between Helen and Joe Waters' irrational fanaticism and Dr. Reed's dispassionate and scholarly analysis of the Bible. Thus a classroom setting, with the stage props of a blackboard, maps, and bright fluorescent lights provides an excellent backdrop to highlight Helen's irrationality. Also, having a formal class in session for Helen and Joe to interrupt by their invasion underscores their unbalanced personalities, and, incidentally, gives a plausible reason for the students present to remain throughout the scene, not simply walk away from this unpleasant encounter, as they would from a scene in the living room.

This outline also requires that the author think about POV. Often, beginning writers ignore this valuable storytelling tool. But by including Point of View on your outline, you must consider assigning the sensory filter before you begin drafting your scenes. In so doing, naturally, you will have to choose your protagonist. Once chosen, the focus of your story will come much easier. And you'd be surprised how many young writers do not know their protagonist when they begin a draft. Notice that Ruth Johnson wisely assigns the POV to Martha, and keeps the focus on her throughout the three scenes of the story.

The action/purpose column of the outline is reasonably straight-forward. But I should say a few words about the *Purpose* subsection. The concept of purpose or function of action is one we discussed earlier. I hope that you'll agree that the function of a story's action and dialogue is to lead characters along a line of conflict that produces tension and is eventually resolved at a pivotal climactic point. In accepting this structure, therefore, you will realize that the events in your scenes must add in some way to the overall purpose of the story (or chapter).

Thus, in "A Contradiction in Terms," the action in scene one is clearly structured to reveal the personalities of Martha and Helen, to dramatize the conflict between them and to foreshadow Martha's eventual violent outburst.

In scene two, the depth of Helen's fanaticism is revealed, and Martha's anger is given another dimension through her acute embarrassment at her roommate's extremism. This embarrassment shows Martha to be less than the serenely tolerant liberal Christian she thought herself to be.

In scene three, the separate elements of Helen's unpredictable faddism and Martha's swelling outrage collide at the explosive pivot of the story. Helen has casually rejected her newfound Christianity and has now embraced the pagan Krishna cult. Martha perceives this as a personal insult. She explodes in a rage that frightens her with its potential for illiberal violence. By the end of the story, the protagonist is profoundly changed; she has learned an unpleasant truth about her own imperfect nature.

Ruth Johnson's outline is a good example of how a writer can keep his energy channeled. With such an outline, a young writer can apply his imagination to the important structural components of dramatic fiction: relevant setting, POV, action and dialogue, conflict, and metaphor. He can also *test* his potential scenes for dramatic impact.

By this, I mean he can examine a series of scenes and decide if they have sufficient conflict and character potential to construct a draft that will hold a reader's interest along a specific line of tension. One of the biggest complaints of college creative writing teachers is that students' stories are bland, lacking in gripping human conflict or—equally problematic—that their stories are empty melodrama, clanking arrays of cataclysmic events completely irrelevant to our normal lives. Fiction, of course, is a shared human experience, but the nature of the experiences the writer chooses to share with his readers is vitally important to the ultimate success or failure of the story.

A writer must choose scenes that are neither too bland to maintain interest nor too sensational to be believed. This balance is one of the skills that comes with time in any writer's career who applies his full intellect to his profession. But the ability to choose your characters and plot events with proper dramatic balance does not simply develop without effort after a requisite number of years toiling in the literary vineyard. You have to think about the problem, and careful outlining will help this rational process.

I've observed during my years teaching fiction writing a marked predilection by young writers to kill off their characters at the end of their stories and novels. That is one extreme. The writers have a hard time completing a rambling draft, so their characters get into trouble—often these days with heavyweight cocaine dealers, it seems—and end up dead. That's one way to resolve the conflict. Alternatively, many amateurs subject the reader to a seemingly endless progression of uneventful scenes in which young husbands and wives talk *ad nauseum* about the difficulty of marriage and the depressing emptiness of modern life. By the end of these boring domestic discussions, one of the spouses usually summons the courage to leave the other and is last observed on a train, plane, bus, or driving the Volvo down the interstate, absolutely ashimmer with ambivalence.

Obviously, there is a middle ground between the extremes of melodrama and the tepid angst reportage that passes for much domestic fiction. Outlining in a scene list helps a writer avoid the extremes. Under the *Purpose* entry, the writer will have to address the problem of meaningful, integrated action. During this stage of the outline, one realizes that the events in a character's life have a function, and that is to show the reader the true nature of this fictional person so that a human experience can be shared.

The *deus ex machina* of a homicidal cocaine dealer who just *happens* to hate the protagonist because their cars once scraped in a parking lot, will not stand up to the dispassionate scrutiny of an outline. An arbitrary murder of a troubled teen-ager is not a valid way to resolve the dramatic conflict between him and his indifferent father. Equally, endless polemical con-versation—punctuated by gratuitous "cigarette" action—does not reveal the troubled human identity of a fictional married couple.

In short, one of the biggest contributions of the scene list outline is that the tool forces us to face the fundamental require-ment of fiction: a believable and compelling human drama, acted out by characters with whom we can share our feelings.

Now that we have examined the role of notetaking and effective outlining, let's look more closely at the actual mechan-ics of rewriting a first draft.

8

Triage of the First Draft
and Story Intent

B Y NOW, we probably all agree that rewriting is important. Many of you will already have begun your personal checklist to help with this vital process. What
I am proposing in this chapter is that you supplement your detailed drafting checklist with another, briefer document. I call this the "Fiction Summary." I used one for several
years, but the questions it raised became so ingrained on me
that I no longer need the tool.

The Fiction Summary sheet is an aid to the process I call
triage—which is, of course, a medical term meaning the separa-
tion of hopelessly injured patients from those who are treatable
in a casualty situation. The summary sheet works the same way:
by the time you've completed the questions, you'll know which
portions of the story or chapter are worth saving, and which are
better cut from the next draft.

FICTION SUMMARY

1. What am I trying to say about the main character or
   characters?
2. What is the *personal* connection between character
   and conflict?

3. How does the character change or what does he learn?

I call this tool a summary because the answer to these three questions provides a handy encapsulation of the entire story or chapter. In applying these questions to a first draft, the writer will quickly expose the irrelevant aspects of the draft, the slack dialogue, the gratuitous action, the meaningless decorative description. These useless elements can be cut by triage.

Moreover, the answers to the three summary questions will provide the writer with a clear objective for the subsequent drafts. Often, when I was redrafting a scene or chapter, I would pin my completed summary sheet onto the cork board that hung at eye level right across the desk from me. That way, I had my rewriting objectives prominently before me as I worked.

Over the years, I've told my students that they should be able to answer each of the summary questions with a single declarative sentence. Let me illustrate this with a model Fiction Summary based on "A Contradiction in Terms."

FICTION SUMMARY

1. What am I trying to say about the main character or characters?
   Martha Phillips is a smug young woman who confuses the trappings of Christianity with compassionate tolerance.

2. What is the personal connection between character and conflict?
   Helen's chaotic religious chameleon act forces Martha to face her own lack of Christian mercy.

3. How does the character change or what does he learn?

> *Martha learns that she has primitive and angry vio-*
> *lence in her personality, despite her veneer of liberal*
> *rationality.*

In answering the three summary questions honestly and completely, the writer learns exactly what these characters and their draft story mean. He can now write the second draft with a specific objective in mind, a firm direction that the finished story should follow. This may sound strange, but—even after careful notetaking and outlining—the writer usually does not understand the true purpose of a scene or story until he has actually written the first draft. As I stressed earlier, your first draft is tangible, you can juggle the words and phrases; you can replace dialogue and metaphor. It is truly your working clay.

Once you have triaged your first draft with the summary questions and you understand what you want to accomplish, you can apply your personal rewriting checklist to the draft. During this process, a lot of ineffective dialogue and irrelevant action will be replaced with more germane material. Cliché will, we hope, vanish, to be replaced by relevant original metaphor. The Pivot of Illumination will be located and suitably intensified, (as in the draft story, "With No Regrets").

Now you are ready for your second draft. And, here I'll suggest yet another rather zany approach to your work. While you are typing out this draft, stop and ask yourself the purpose of the changes you've made. I don't mean that you should silently wonder in a vague manner why your characters now speak in a certain way. What I'm suggesting is that you stop and ask yourself these questions *out loud.*

"Does this dialogue sound more like Helen?"

"Is this metaphor related to Martha's mood?"

Why out loud? Am I trying to embarrass you before your roommates?

Not at all; I'm simply trying to get you to slow down and think about what you're doing.

You create an interesting metaphoric phrase. Ask yourself, "Is this trite?"

By stopping your stream of activity and speaking aloud (a whisper will suffice), you break the pseudo-creative trance that many writers feel they must enter before they produce imaginative material.

You've completed your second draft. Now what? The first thing I'd suggest is to put the draft in a large manila envelope (the kind with a brass fastener and a glued flap), seal it, and lock the envelope in a desk drawer for at least five days. This cooling off period is something we all need. Without the dispassionate perspective that can only come with time, we won't be able to judge the effectiveness of the draft.

If you don't literally lock away your draft, the temptation to pick at it (like a scab on your knee) will be too strong to resist. But once the five days have passed, you'll have some distance from the words. Now you can employ one of two interesting critical approaches. First, if you have a close friend in whom you can confide and from whom you can reasonably expect honesty, you can ask this friend to read you the second draft out loud. In this manner, you will hear the tone and flow of the story from a fresh vantage point. The well-constructed dialogue and metaphor will be obvious; equally, the clumsy areas will be prominent. If you aren't comfortable with this approach, record the draft as you read it aloud yourself, then listen to the recording without the manuscript before you.

Take notes as you listen to the reading. If dialogue is too long, note the need to cut it. If a character's action is not truly relevant to mood, make a note to replace it. Be ruthless. When in doubt, cut and mold. Your second draft is far from the end product. Please note that I only recommend listening without the manuscript before you at this stage so that you will actually hear the flow of words, and not get caught up in the storyline.

Now, read the draft again, slowly, aloud to yourself. Use your rewriting checklist to monitor dialogue and action. Highlight each metaphor and critically assess if it is trite and if it is appropriate for the tone you intend for this section of the draft. Check for inadvertent sentence pattern repetition and awkwardly repeated words and phrases. Circle the entire pivot point with a colored pen. Ask yourself if it works the way you had intended. If not, sit down at your typewriter and reconstruct it.

At this stage of the drafting process a handy Xerox machine and a pair of scissors are very helpful. Cut-and-pasting from draft two to draft three can be a lot of fun, and the exercise will give you the confidence that you are in control of your own work, *you,* the craftsman, not some intangible force like inspiration. I've discovered in the past couple years that a word processor is an invaluable tool at this stage of cut-and-paste drafting, and I've devoted part of a chapter to using the word processor in fiction writing. But many of you will want to stick with a typewriter and your personal checklist for the immediate future. Word processors can come later in your career.

Let's review these stages of the drafting process. You've applied the triage of the Fiction Summary, then let your first draft cool off for several days. Next you've listened for awkward and ineffective passages and corrected these problems, using your rewriting checklist. Now you are ready to type up a clean third draft and show your work to readers outside your immediate circle of friends. In short, you're about to face the emotional gauntlet of criticism. There's not much I can say to make the process pleasant. But in the next chapter I can at least offer suggestions that will channel the painful process along constructive lines.

9

Critique and Self-Improvement:
Specific Goals
from Draft to Draft

OFTEN a young writer's work is first critiqued in a creative writing class or fiction workshop. I think that my opinion on the overall efficacy of these groups is clear to you by now. Most writing classes and workshops that I have observed are less than one hundred percent effective. The peer-review of student work, in particular, is usually a slipshod, undirected process that often degenerates into a popularity contest and sniping session; rarely does the student writer receive *practical* editorial guidance.

Let me offer some possible techniques to improve the effectiveness of manuscript criticism. First, the manuscript itself should be reproduced, so that every member of the group has a Xeroxed copy of the draft to be discussed, at least three days before the scheduled discussion. I've seen many creative writing classes in which a writer will simply read a draft story to the group, then ask for comments. Naturally enough, these comments are usually in the "I like it," or "it's nice" range of critical acuity. The group has no opportunity to closely examine the draft with a craftsman's perspective.

In my classes and workshops, the individual writer is responsible for copying the draft under discussion, in sufficient numbers so that the entire group has the manuscript, several days before the planned critique. With this manuscript, the writer also must provide a brief statement of what he intended to accomplish in the draft. Naturally, this statement is a close approximation of the Fiction Summary he's used to check his first draft.

The discussion, therefore, has a structure and a purpose. And the participants in the critique are now required to address the specific points raised by the writer's statement of intent. For example, a writer might state that he intended his draft story to dramatize the revulsion felt by Dan Palmer, a young Army enlisted man during the frustrating final months of America's presence in Vietnam. The motives for this frustration, the author states, are combined guilt, fear and anger at the seemingly dishonest American strategists in Saigon.

Fine, that is his intent. Let's say that the critique group receives the draft of "With No Regrets" and the author's brief statement. In planning the discussion for the next class meeting, I would then ask two members to form a team to specifically comment on the author's intent and on how well he accomplished it. Beyond that responsibility, they would be required to make concrete, *practical* suggestions on how the author could correct the major problems of the draft—in this case the lack of dramatized motive.

Next, I would assign one person each the responsibility of discussing . . . you guessed it:

> Believable and Relevant Physical Setting
> Effectiveness of Point of View
> Relevant Dramatic Action
> Relevant Dialogue
> Relevant Descriptive Metaphor

In each case the class member selected would be required to find both the specific problems and offer detailed, practical suggestions for the rewrite of the draft. Thus the discussion would be a structured and focused examination of the author's intention, how well he met that stated goal in this draft, and, most importantly, how he might specifically improve the next draft. This method avoids lazy generalities and superficial reading.

There are a number of advantages to this approach. First, the writer realizes that he must understand his own intention for the story. He avoids the formless, undisciplined outpouring of unconnected characters and free-floating metaphor—the so-called "mood piece" or "abstract sketch" that passes for dramatic fiction in so many creative writing classes. If a writer knows his work will receive such close, structured scrutiny he will work harder to shape his draft.

Another clear advantage to this method concerns the Emperor's New Clothes syndrome I mentioned earlier. The teacher and class members alike are now required to carefully analyze the draft under discussion. Vague comments (often based on a cursory reading of the manuscript) are no longer acceptable. Certain members of the group will have more specific responsibility. They must think hard about craft in practical terms. Is this dialogue exchange believable or "Bob and Ray"? What more relevant actions can the author add in the rewrite to replace this "cigarette action" in paragraph three of page two? Is there a connection between these trite descriptions at the bottom of the page and the mood the author wants to build here? How can the chichés be replaced with relevant metaphor? Do you have specific examples?

With this disciplined critical method, everyone learns from the exercise, not just the person whose work is under discussion, but also the group members, and the teacher, as well. I can honestly say that I learned more about the practical matters of fiction-writing craft during the first two years I taught the subject than I did during my first five years as a professional writer.

One more positive element of the structured group critique

is that the dispassionate, analytical approach tends to ease the embarrassment and anxiety of the person whose work is under discussion. All of us hate to have our material ripped apart. There is a cruel paradox in creative people that compels them to expose their work—a story, a painting, or a song—to their peers for critical comment, knowing full well that the process is the emotional equivalent of surgery without anesthesia. I've seen people become physically weak when their drafts have been criticized in a workshop. Others have become belligerent to the threshold of physical violence when someone speaks frankly about an ineffective draft novel chapter.

Clearly, this volatile emotional atmosphere is not conducive to what people insist on calling "a good learning experience." If your blood pressure is topping out at 240 over 110 or your gastric muscles are convulsed to the point of rupture, you are hardly likely to listen carefully to your colleagues' comments. And, let's be painfully frank while we're at it. Many people in fiction workshops, both young and old, use their comments as blackmail currency. If you cut down my piece, the perverted logic goes, I'll sure as hell repay you in kind. The first couple of classes I taught, I encountered this nasty process, and I decided to structure my manuscript discussions in a way to avoid the unproductive and immature rivalry.

If you are not now, never have been, nor ever intend to be, a member of a formally structured group such as a university creative writing class, you can still take advantage of the structured draft-to-draft critique process described in this chapter. A small, informal group of friends can make good use of the method. In reality, a discussion group with as few as two people can also benefit. What you really need is the logical, structured approach, not large numbers of participants.

For example, you and your spouse are both interested in fiction writing; one writes novels, the other science fiction stories. The formal critical process will serve to defuse the implied personal criticism, the rejection-failure perception, that often accompanies criticism. My story is a failure, therefore I'm a flop, and you don't love me. If you think I'm exaggerating, teach a fiction workshop with married couples in it.

I will readily admit that everyone interested in writing fiction will not profit equally from the emotional distancing this critical method provides. Some people seem so personally connected to their work, that any criticism whatsoever, no matter how logically structured, well-intended and fairly administered, throws them into an angry, defensive depression. Such people will invariably go to baroque lengths to defend a snatch of clumsy dialogue or an irrelevant setting detail. They will protest when no personal criticism was implied. And, in my experience, they rarely learn as much craft as their colleagues who more-or-less cheerfully enter the process.

Defending the indefensible is one side of the coin (cliché! I hear you all exclaim). The other is slavishly building predictable, set-piece dramatic structure in which each scene opens with a named character using tightly focused POV to sense stage props, which then trigger internal monologue and reveal conflict. In other words, mindless attempts to *replicate* the exact structure of the rewritten "A Contradiction in Terms" or "With No Regrets" is just as undisciplined, in my opinion, as belligerently rationalizing for clichés and stilted dialogue. There is a vast middle ground in which most successful writers find their own comfortable style, their own favorite structural format.

I want to emphasize that my sacred Five Components of the Well-Integrated Fictional Scene are analogous to the chemical requisites of organic molecules. As we learn in high school chemistry, all organic compounds require carbon and hydrogen, but the way these elements are *arranged* in the molecule completely alters the nature of the compound. Dimethyl ether and ethyl alcohol have equal amounts of carbon, hydrogen and oxygen, don't they? But they are not aligned identically along the molecule's valence axis. If you don't think this changes the flavor of the compound, try replacing the alcohol with ether in a bottle of *grand cru* 1948 Chateau Rothschild-Mouton and see what you get.

What I mean by this analogy is that a writer can pay proper attention to the fictional craft elements in brilliantly original ways. In fact, all the knowledge of integrated fictional structure in the world will not help you write imaginative, original fiction unless you learn to employ your imagination in an original manner.

And that is, interestingly enough, our next subject of discussion.

10

Original Perception and
Training the Imagination

IMAGINATION, the dictionary tells us, is "the act or power of creating mental images of what has never been actually experienced, or of creating new images or ideas by combining previous experiences."

Some of us seem to have been born with more imagination than others, but we all have the ability to imagine to a certain extent. I think that the capacity to form mental images, to project vivid cerebral drama, is an evolutionary skill that human beings acquired with consciousness. Most so-called higher mammals dream—we've all seen the whimpering dog with legs atwitch, snoring away before the fireplace, while his mind hunts rabbits. But only *Homo sapiens* seem able to create dreamlike drama when awake. Thus early man, two thousand centuries ago, could gaze at a dark tree line and *see* the sabre-toothed tiger lurking in ambush for the foraging party about to leave the open savanna for the dangerous forest. Imagination, in other words, helped us survive where other species became extinct.

Being able to sense the intangible, and then to reshape and recreate the image on demand has permitted our frail species to master abstract thought, tool-making and symbolic language, and, using these uniquely combined human attributes, to become the planet's dominant life form.

As fiction writers, imagination is to craft as a good ear for pitch is to the musician or color sensitivity is to the painter. Without a readily available imagination, a skill that he can exercise every day, the amateur writer is faced with the unpleasant and difficult task of activating his imagination from a cold start whenever he sits down to draft a scene. We must exercise this vital tool regularly or it becomes stiff and clumsy from disuse. Unfortunately, most young writers I've met only trot out their imaginations when faced with the actual challenge of drafting. They did not learn as children to train their imaginations, to practice forming images "of what has never been actually experienced."

When I teach a fiction writing seminar, I can always recognize the work of those over forty, who grew up without television and spent years listening to the radio. "The Lone Ranger," "The Green Hornet," and, of course, "The Shadow" ("While in the Orient, Lamont Cranston learned the power to cloud men's minds"), might have seemed inconsequential entertainment to our parents, but, to us, those richly evocative radio dramas were the catalyst for imaginative projections that few members of the television generation experienced in childhood.

Unfortunately, television is fully revealed drama. What you see is what you get, one hundred percent. The screen is filled with a living scene, and viewing requires no involvement. In my opinion, television stifles imagination by its very opulence of dramatic image. In a fractional second, the screen fills with sharply focused color and action. A physical setting rich with artfully contrived detail, characters with all their individually tailored quirks of appearance and voice, and the myriad other elements that weave dramatic tapestry, are flashed at us with electronic speed. Television assaults and conquers our senses; we surrender to its presence, but cannot participate. As McLuhan proclaimed, the medium is, indeed, cool.

Radio drama, however, forced the listener to participate, to people the invisible scene with *imagined* characters, to project a face to match a voice, a setting for the sound effects, and mood in response to dialogue nuance. As we lay on the living room rug, curled up before the varnished bulk of the Zenith, Sky King and Dale acted out their dramatic lives in an imaginary mental landscape. The dark, echoing streets and alleys in which Boston Blackie confronted assorted mobsters, kidnappers and Nazi spies, existed only in our minds—not in living color on a twenty-four-inch stage. Our true radio stage was juvenile imagination, and on it we first learned to project character, setting, dialogue and dramatic action.

But I do not want to waste time with nostalgic gloating. Rather, I'd like to simply state that dramatic imagination used to be enhanced by radio drama in childhood. But if you feel you've been shortchanged by a childhood of "Star Trek" and "Gilligan's Island," there's no need to despair. It is never too late to exercise and develop that unique human attribute, imagination.

First, you must consider what the exact function of imagination is in effective dramatic fiction. This may seem obvious, but I've found that many young writers have developed the compound bad habit of overly literal perception and compulsively nihilistic melodrama. By this I mean that they employ the flat, neutral descriptive language of the Anglo-Saxon verbs—"Jason walked into the room, sat down, looked out the window and saw that the neighborhood was . . . " *Walk, sat, look, see,* the flat products of unimaginative, literal perception. The compulsion for nihilistic melodrama often accompanies this dry "stick-man" action, " . . . and saw that the neighborhood was filling up with armed police. He was trapped. He lit a cigarette, then took his .38 and put an end to his miserable existence, another victim of so-called *recreational* drugs."

Let's see what we actually have in this exaggerated passage. Obviously, the writer was unable to develop an effective sensory filter of character POV—the line is utterly devoid of sensory detail or metaphoric description. Also, the lifeless generic verbs give us no information about Jason's emotions. Amateur writers employ these static verbs, they tell me, because they cannot truly imagine their characters; in other words, they have not learned to act out the drama in their minds, to hear Jason's muddy running shoes slip on the cracked linoleum of the old apartment stairs, to feel him sink, shaking with panic, to the edge of the broken Naugehide recliner, etc., etc.

The character they envision is what I call a "stick man," not a fully fleshed fictional person. Because this inability to project three-dimensional imaginary characters inhibits the writer's narrative range, he often feels compelled to employ apocalyptic *(deus ex machina)* conclusions to his plots. Thus we find sterile stick-man characters jumping off buildings, driving cars into telephone poles or suicidally cutting loose with an M–16 at a crowded sidewalk—all spectacular, but unconvincing dooms-day methods of stopping a lifeless story.

Once the writer learns to sense his characters as breathing, feeling people, however, he can develop human conflicts that reach appropriate and believable resolutions. This doesn't mean that he is prevented from weaving intensely emotional events into his stories. These events, however, will be drama-tized by characters with whom the reader can share experi-ence, if the writer also shares that experience.

I'm sometimes frustrated as a teacher when I encounter a writer who seems incapable or unwilling to ride with the imagi-nary thrust of a story. For example, if he brings me a draft scene in which the setting and characters lack sensory detail, then throws up his hands when I ask what color the walls are in the kitchen. This was actually the problem once in a story confer-ence at Purdue. The draft was flat; there was no attempt to integrate setting with character, or action and emotional con-flict. I asked the student to describe the apartment kitchen in which the scene took place. "It's just a kitchen," he muttered.

"What kind of floor does it have? What color are the walls?"

The young man gazed at me as if I were mentally unbalanced. "I don't know what you mean," he said, frowning. "It doesn't *have* any floor or walls. It's just in a *story.*"

Although he didn't realize the true meaning of his words, the young man was admitting that his powers of imaginative perception and projection were so stunted that he was unable to visualize even a relatively familiar domestic setting. Moreover, this student was clearly embarrassed by my efforts to stimulate his imagination. I think that he felt there was something inherently weak or dishonest about the ability to envision nonexistent people and settings.

A few weeks later, he dropped the course and I lost track of him. Natural selection, I guess. He was equipped with neither storytelling experience nor the desire to acquire the minimum imaginative perception to develop as a writer. I remember that he found my imagination-training exercises especially galling, and refused to enter the spirit of the process with the rest of the class.

These exercises and their numerous variations, however, are simple and amusing, and I can guarantee that they work. One of the first assignments I offer in a young writer's effort to expand his imagination is what I call "controlled eavesdropping." The writer is told to station himself in a crowded public place—the dining room of a dormitory or a cafeteria line will do well—and there select two people engaged in conversation. He is to eavesdrop unobserved for as long as practically possible, then retire and make notes on the overheard conversation.

Next, the writer is asked to create a dramatic biography in outline form, based on what he managed to glean from the conversation. Clearly, there will not be enough valid data in the few minutes of conversation to provide an accurate biographical sketch. He therefore has to invent the details of these randomly selected people's lives. While in the process, of course, the people are transformed from real human beings into fictional characters. The major advantage of this exercise is that the writer has no problem visualizing his characters and hearing their voices. After all, he's been standing next to them in the cafeteria line and eavesdropping on their lunch conversation for fifteen minutes. The writer stretches his imagination to construct fictional characters who are built up from brief surreptitious observation. This exercise can be repeated as often as needed to help fledgling writers.

Another exercise I employ is what I've come to call building "ironic perspective." By this term I mean the ability to perceive mundane events or objects and then to describe them in ironic terms. Irony, I always explain to those students unfamiliar with the term, is defined as "an unexpected reversal of expected meaning, often for purposes of emphasis." Thus, an ironic speaker calls a nonsensical statement "very astute." But, for this exercise the ironic description is dependent on the writer's imaginative capacity to perceive the normal in an unexpected manner.

I'll show the class a supposedly commonplace object and ask them to examine it with ironic perspective. What, I'll ask, is the *true* essence of this item: Put yourself in the POV of an extraterrestial space traveler. You've never seen such a thing before. Perhaps we have a bouquet of flowers, just normal offerings from the florist's cooler, a few tulips, daisies or half a dozen roses. Paraphrasing Gertrude Stein, I state, "A rose is a rose is a flower. But what is a flower?"

A flower, I'm usually told, is, well, it's just a flower. But sometimes, there'll be a young person who is beginning to understand the exercise.

"A flower," one girl told me with mixed embarrassment and pride at her imaginative insight, "is the reproductive organ of the plant."

Bingo! "A rose is a rose is the genitals of R. Rosacease."

Now, we're getting somewhere. All those pretty blossoms the Victorian ladies used to decorate their parlors were, in fact, so much colorfully erect genital tissue, the plant kingdom's equivalent of a baboon's backside. Nobody would really deny this, but few *normal* people would see a bouquet of violets as plant pornography. Absolutely. But nobody ever said writers were supposed to see the world as normal people do. *Au contraire, mon ami.*

For example. Dan Palmer, the disgruntled Army flyer in DaNang, observes the "green velvet scum" in the ditch beside the flightline. Nice metaphoric image, but is this the observation of a balanced, decent young man? Hell, no. And Dan was none of those things when he made that observation.

Wait, you say. *Dan* didn't observe this, the writer did. Okay, now you're getting the idea.

One very important action of fictional characters is that they perceive their world ironically. And, in order for this to occur, their writer-creators must do the same.

When the medic peeled back the dead man's poncho to reveal the "rippling curd of pus," he was not seeing his world in a sane, detached manner. That is the ironic perspective of a deeply troubled person. And that's exactly what the writer intended to dramatize about this character.

We must *practice* on a daily basis looking at the world around us in an original and ironic (i.e. unexpected) metaphoric manner. This is what writers do. Ruth Johnson saw Helen's cluttered desk as a "wrecked truck." Strange way to see it, huh? You bet. And also quite effective.

One student whom I originally thought had little potential charmed me with this description of a crowd entering the Seventh Avenue subway: "The line sagged between the green teeth of the railings. People freely entered this hole in the earth, apparently unaware of the millions of tons of rock and metal about to snap shut above their heads." Not bad at all.

Another girl described a flight to California. "We sat silently in narrow ranks, drinking alcohol from tiny bottles, six miles above dark Kentucky."

How about, "The nurse bristled into the sunny room, static aggression sparking from her starched shoulders"?

We must learn to perceive the normal world in weird original ways; that is what I call ironic perspective.

One way you can practice this skill is to acquire the discipline of assigning yourself exercises to expand your own imaginative perceptions. For example, take two weeks during which you will write five ironically original descriptions of normal events and objects every day. Stick it out; work at it. This is not a game, but professional training.

A quarter-pounder becomes "Two-hundred twenty-seven grams of heat-degraded muscle tissue from an immature, castrated male bovine."

A milkshake is transformed into "The mammary secretions of the female of the same species, emulsified with the unfertilized germ cell of a domestic fowl."

Kind of turns you off your lunch, right? But, what if you had an anorexic character and you wanted to describe her view of a meal at MacDonald's?

There is a wonderfully original Canadian novelist, whose name has disappeared from my memory, who once wrote what I consider to be a brilliant example of ironic perception. I hate to paraphrase, but I think the writer wouldn't mind in this case.

A character is strolling down a Toronto sidewalk when he spies a plastic dog turd in the window of a novelty store. The character stops, realizes what he's looking at and ponders the artifact. Slowly, his perception widens; he realizes that this piece of plastic, like all plastic items, has come from some kind of metal mold. In turn, the mold had to be made from a casting, the casting designed by normal, adult engineers and draftsmen, the entire manufacturing process subject to the corporate world's banalities of budgets and deadlines. As his ironic insight expands, he peoples it with a group of normal, middle-class workers and executives who arrive at the firm each day at eight A.M., sit down at their drawing boards and desks and undertake the serious business of manufacturing and selling plastic dog excrement.

That, I offer, is a prime piece of ironic and original perception. The world surrounding us is replete with similar oddities. But we have to open our imaginations to see the splendid opportunities that make up the fabric of our daily lives. A rose isn't just a rose.

Sometimes I will goad my students' imaginations by forcing them to confront the underlying absurdity of human existence. This is good for all writers; it keeps our senses attuned to the commonplace mysteries. Usually I'll pick on some poor young person who happens to be in my line of sight when the thought occurs.

"How much do you weigh?" I'll ask a startled sophomore in cashmere sweater and proud new sorority pin.

After an embarrassed pause, she'll reply, "One hundred and twenty pounds."

"How old are you?"

"Nineteen."

"All right, you're nineteen and you weigh one hundred and twenty pounds. Tell me this: How much did you weigh twenty-one years ago?"

If a class could have a collective expression of stupefied alarm, they usually produce it at this point.

"I . . . don't know what you mean?"

"This is serious!" I bluster. "I want an answer. Today you weigh one hundred and twenty pounds, but what was your weigh on March 4, 1964?"

"I didn't weigh *any*thing. I wasn't even. . . . "

"No excuses!" I shout. "I need answers. How much will you weight on March 4, 2100?"

At this point, the group is getting my point.

"I won't weigh anything. I'll be gone."

"So," I proclaim, "You expect me to *believe* this nonsense. You're sitting here in a green sweater and gray pleated skirt, digesting your lunch, taking notes on your pad, clearly a healthy human being, yet you expect me to believe that only twenty-

one years ago you didn't weigh *anything?* And worse," I bel-
low, "you claim that you're going to just disappear in a hundred
and fifteen years, that nobody's going to be able to locate you,
no matter how hard they search? Is *that* what you expect me
to believe?"

The young woman nods, her embarrassment dissolving.

"You people think *I'm* weird," I mutter, shaking my head,
"yet you call something like *that* normal."

Usually, one such session is enough to show young writers
that they must learn to examine the universe around them from
a fresh perspective.

And, once they adopt this new vantage point, they must use
it on a daily basis. I encourage the most flagrant, and, I'll admit,
sometimes erotic daydreams. I actually invite serious engineering and computer science students to turn their backs on the
normal world of equations and velocity tables and examine the
hidden fabric of the world.

Simon and Garfunkel (remember them?) had a sixties song
in which two young vagabonds played "games with faces" of
fellow passengers on a Greyhound. The man in the gabardine
suit is a spy, etc. Such games, I maintain, are about as silly and
slothful as a Warega child on Zaire's Lualaba river "playing"
with a small bow and arrow. When that kid grows up, the bow
will bring meat to the family pot. When a young writer decides
to turn professional, his ability to imaginatively project believable characters will be the means by which he pays the rent.

Here's one way to find interesting characters. You can go
into any public place, but I'm especially partial to bars and
restaurants with tables near a sidewalk window. There you can
sit with a beer or a mug of coffee and observe the flow of people
without being noticed. Let your consciousness drift with the
traffic, but be alert for people of potential interest. Take notes
on the good ones. That attractive young woman in designer
jeans has become a call girl to support her dying father. (Not to

be sexist, take the guy in the jogging suit and make him a gigolo.) The old lady with the orthopedic shoe is actually a con woman, about to make a hit at the savings and loan down the block. The young policeman lounging in his patrol car across the street plays in a rock band at night and is carrying $6,000 in illegal drug money in his jacket pocket.

You can let your list expand for hours, if you're so inclined. Now, however, the supposedly idle daydreams acquire some substance. Examine your list of colorful characters whom you've created from the unsuspecting passersby. Eliminate the melodramatic extremes, then write a scene-list story outline for the remaining characters. Naturally, you'll have to employ the five components of effective dramatic fiction in this outline to make the exercise worthwhile. You may not have time to actually draft a story from the outlines, but you'll have sharpened your skills of dramatic imagination in the process.

Another valuable tool to expand your imagination is a natural spin-off of the preceding exercise. Instead of you writing the story from the scene-list outline, trade outlines with someone who has undergone the same process of character observation and creation. Often, you'll find that you've been given a character whose profession and social position are totally alien to you. Let's say that a young writer very interested in military aviation gives you a plot that concerns a Navy carrier pilot who is trying to hide the existence of a brain tumor from the flight surgeon. For this writer, the subject is quite familiar, but for you, the characters might as well be from another planet.

What do you do, give up? I'd suggest, instead, that you accept the challenge and learn to do some basic fictional research. There is plenty already written about naval aviators; any good librarian can lead you to the books and documents. A Navy recruiting office can give you enough background to build believable and relevant settings. The medical library at any university will provide adequate background to write about the brain tumor. In short, there's no valid excuse for rejecting the idea.

But, you say, I don't *want* to write about these characters. I want to write stories about people I know.

Of course you do. Everyone does. But how many stories about college sophomores or discontent housewives get published every year? You have to learn to let your imagination expand to encompass exotic (for you, at least) characters and conflict situations. Maybe the naval pilot simply doesn't appeal to you as a person. How about taking the story then from the POV of a civilian woman neurologist who's been brought in by the flight surgeon for a second opinion?

Still, many young writers will resist. *I just don't know anything about medicine.* And, as Hemingway once said, and every high school creative writing teacher on the continent has since echoed, you should only write about what you know. But that would mean that a man can *never* write from the POV of a woman character, right? And vice versa. Or that a writer born wealthy would have to squander the family fortune before he could people his novel with Latino migrant workers, right?

Wrong. The next logical step beyond the imagination expansion and ironic perspective exercises I've described here is learning the skills of fictional research.

If, for example, you are determined to place the action of your story in Miami, but you've never been there, I can suggest several courses of action. First, examine the dramatic potential of Miami in your characters' conflict. What aspects of the city are truly relevant to the characters' lives? You'll find, I think, that the entire megalopolis of Greater Miami is not essential to the story. Probably only the beachfront hotels, for example, and the live-aboard colony at a nearby marina. This selectivity, based on your outline, allows you to narrow the range of your research.

Unless you have extra time and money, you don't have to travel all the way to Miami. The overall geography of the city can be obtained from a good road atlas, a Xeroxed encyclopedia entry, and some chamber of commerce literature. But you need to get a better collection of sensory setting details from a resort hotel and the atmosphere of the marina. How do you do that if you're stuck in Omaha? Here's where your imagination comes to the fore. Even in landlocked Nebraska, good magazine stores carry *Yachting, SAIL,* and *Cruising World.* These sailing periodicals have lots of pictures of boats in Florida marinas. There's a wealth of accurate, specific detail, as well as the specific names of boat models in these magazines. Further, by consulting the Guide to Periodical Literature at the library, you can find articles that discuss the merits of living aboard your boat in a marina. If your library is large enough, you'll even find books on the subject. Armed with this material, you can create enough accurate and believable setting detail to support an effective dramatic story.

But, what about the beachfront resort hotel setting? Well, hotel management is a widely practiced profession. There are several good professional journals in the hotel industry and a variety of books on the subject. Also, you can telephone resorts on toll-free 800 numbers to request slick, four-color advertising brochures to supplement those available at your local travel agent. As with the marina background material, the Miami Beach brochures should provide ample detail for you to create the setting of your story.

But accurate graphic material alone won't automatically give the story an authentic and relevant tone. Vividness, after-all, comes from the adjective "vivid," doesn't it? Which, of course, comes from the Latin *vivere,* to live. So, for your stories to actually come alive, you must carefully employ Point of View, that important sensory filter. You must use your increasing powers of imagination to get inside your character's body, to sense the setting details through his sight, hearing, touch, smell, and taste.

You know from the maps that there's a causeway connecting

Miami Beach with Key Biscayne, and that there's a marina on the ocean side of the causeway. You study the photographs and make notes on the palmetto trees, the clapboard bait shops, the vast parking lots of hot, shimmering cars. This is all good stuff, but it's not truly *vivid*. Then, you make an imaginative leap.

You actually enter your character's skin. It's sunset, the tide is out. Across the bay, the highrise clutter of downtown is silhouetted, smoggy peach. A halyard pings against an alloy mast. Beneath your bare feet, the sunwarped boards of the dock are still hot. As the tide falls, slick, weedy pilings appear, and you smell the iodine bite of the polluted bay. Suddenly, it is humid night, and mosquitos merge with the whining ski boats returning from their last runs.

How, you ask, can a person write with this degree of POV detail without actually knowing a place? By combining document research with imaginative projection, that's how. I've never been to a marina in Miami. But I know how to read, and, most importantly, I've taught my imagination to carry my senses to exotic places.

And, with a little practice, you can travel this way as well.

11

Vivid Imagery and Mood
Enhancement

I MAGERY is one of these academic terms that scares amateur writers. There is implied artistry in the word, and
hints of inexplicable genius. We all learn in literature
classes to appreciate, indeed, to marvel at the well-
crafted metaphoric images of The Great Authors. But aspiring
writers sit there in class thinking, "How the hell am *I* supposed
to pull off something like this?" We are taught, for example, that
Hemingway's Italian soldiers marching up to the front, whose
capes bulge over their ammunition pouches "like women seven
months gone with child," are an elegant foreshadowing of preg-
nancy and death later to merge in *A Farewell to Arms*.

Wow! we mutter, how on earth is *any* body supposed to plan
so far in advance? I can never come up with a trick like *that*.

Well, as far as I know, Ernest Hemingway didn't, either. He
rewrote the opening chapter of the novel after the first draft
was complete. So, he knew that the heroine, Catherine, was
going to die in childbirth in the final chapter when he sat down
to do his rewrite. Now, I can't guarantee that he consciously
decided to include a merged gestation-death image on the first
page of chapter one, but I'm confident that the concepts of
birth and violent death were on his mind as he began to reshape
the manuscript.

But Hemingway's a Great Author, you say. You're just a

beginner, and you simply can't come up with such intricate fictional tapestries, replete with foreshadowing and mood-conflict connections.

Maybe, but none of us simply "comes up" with these elegant craft pirouettes. Most of our early drafts contain either flat, incomplete metaphoric description, or, all too often, trite images and clichés. By the third draft, however, we tend to understand the story much better, and we are able to tinker carefully with the descriptive passages.

I like to believe that was what old Papa Hemingway did with his dusty soldiers' capes swelling across the leather ammunition pouches. He was certainly a careful writer, and Gertrude Stein had browbeat him long enough about craft to cause him to consider his images with great care as he made the fine adjustments to his draft.

We'll never know for sure what motivated that particular image. But I do know that here, today, even beginning writers can learn to create original and effective image patterns that enhance the mood of their work with truly professional elegance. Let's examine this second-draft story, "At the Tel-way."

"At the Tel-way"
(Second Draft)
by Susan Warne

The young waitress tapped the register keys, practicing the touch with the dry sides of her finger tips. She didn't want to break another nail. The crimson enamel was chipped off her forefinger, but so far today her nails were still intact.

Her shift had started at three, and since then no one had come into the Tel-way for a hamburger. Bored, she leaned back against the count-

er and started counting the red-and-white
tiles on the floor. She considered stepping on
a pale brown ant. Instead, she marveled at how
well her white uniform set off her country club
tan. Still, she had to admit that the white lost
most of its appeal off the tennis courts. Maybe
it was just that everything lost its appeal at
the Tel-way.

She was more than a little annoyed that her
father had insisted on "the responsibility" of
this summer job. It would help her maintain perspective, he had said. She was a little less
than angry, though, since it was only for
fifteen hours a week.

The Tel-way had three glass walls and a
kitchen to the back. She could watch the movement of people in every direction except from
the north. Everyday it was the same. The old
gentleman would come from the north and check
the restroom door. It was always locked.
Pressing his palm against the window, he
proceeded around the building with an
equilibrium that rivaled a far more sober man.

She still jumped when the hand would appear
on the glass. She stared as it moved, followed
by a smearing film and unsure feet on the
ground. But the shoulders were steady. His chin
was level, tilted ever so slightly, to assure
that the next step was properly placed. She had
never seen him trip.

Everyday it was the same. At the door, he
drew a full breath, reached for the handle and

pulled it open by throwing his weight back-
wards. Then he let go and walked through as if
it were being held open for him. She waited for
the day when the door would slam into his heel,
chopping the vulnerable Achilles tendon.

It took him only three strides to reach her
at the cash register, but he always relied on
the counter to stop his forward motion. When he
spoke, the folds in his face opened to show the
nicks of a dulling razor. There seemed to be a
new nick each day.

"Cup a coffee, cream please." The request
was more of a petition than an order.

The huge khaki pants were belted high above
his waistline, forcing him to raise his elbow
in an awkward, almost grotesque, way when he
pulled the change from his pocket.

"Would you like that to go?"

"That would be fine."

She snapped the plastic lid on the coffee
and took his moist array of nickels and pennies. After ringing the sale, she wiped her
hands on her red apron. It was an odd reaction,
but she caught herself doing it each time the
old man left the Tel-way.

It was the same everyday. He would lean on
the rusty green trash bin in the parking lot and
swallow the hot coffee in three gulps. He carefully placed the empty container in the bin and
returned for another cup, repeating his narrow
miss with the door and his sudden halt at the
counter.

"Cup a coffee, cream please."

"Would you like that to go?"

"That would be fine."

As he reached for his money, he asked, "Lavatory open today?"

"Was the door locked?"

"Yes."

She took her eyes from him as she dropped the coins in the register. "Guess it's not open then."

"Thank you."

She decided that the alcohol had not only increased his natural urges, but dulled his sense. She probably would have opened the toilet for him if he had asked, but he never would.

He drank the second cup at the trash bin, deposited the empty, and moved south, using the parked cars the same way he had used the windows at the Tel-way.

Wiping her hands on her apron, she thought that tomorrow she would tell him that refills were free if a person ordered coffee to stay. Then again, maybe she wouldn't. She gazed at the smeared window and lightly tapped her nails on the register keys.

Everyday it was the same.

When Susan Warne brought me the first draft of this story, she was a senior in Chemical Engineering at Purdue. Susan hadn't had a great deal experience writing, but as an engineering student, she was used to learning a lot of complex information in a short period. If the story had promise, she told me, she wanted to enter it in the literary awards competition, the deadline of which was only ten days off.

Fine, I said, reaching for my yellow highlighter and red felt pen. Once I'd indicated the normal problems of awkward phrasing, inadvertent word and sentence-pattern repetition and a few clichés, I asked her to think about mood and image. This story, I stressed, depended much more on subtle mood than intense dramatic action for its impact. The potential of the setting-situation, after all, did not provide for a truly deep emotional exchange between the bored young waitress and the old alcoholic. Therefore the human experience that this piece of fiction was offering the reader to share would have to arise from dramatic components other than dialogue and physical action. By this I meant that it was implausible that the drunken old man and the upper-class student-waitress could realistically interact through conversation or relevant dramatic action.

Using the Fiction Summary approach, I asked Susan to answer the first question: What am I trying to say about the main character?

As any good scientist, she carefully considered her answer. "The girl is so selfishly egocentric," Susan finally said, "that she can feel no compassion for the old man. She considers him less than human, almost like the ant on the floor, like a . . ."

". . . Like a bug," I said. "Look at this line on page two."

"She still jumped when the palm would appear on the glass," Susan read. "She stared as it moved, followed by a smearing film and unsure feet on the ground."

Susan dropped the page and frowned; I saw she did not fully understand the relevance of this passage to her overall intent.

"What kind of bug leaves a smeared trail, a slimy film behind it?" I asked.

"Snails," she said. "Or those yucky slugs that eat the roses."

"So, your young country club waitress sees the old man as

a repulsive slug. Isn't that another way of answering my Fiction Summary question?"

Susan agreed, and we set to work to locate places in the draft where the slug image could be intensified. A consciously intensified image pattern, I explained, is a series of specific metaphors and descriptions that link to create a mood. This is a device that works without the writer resorting to the intrusion of a Loudspeaker narrator.

In the first paragraph of the draft, Susan added the adjective "dry" to describe the girl's finger tips. This might seem an irrelevant addition, but on page three she then changed "took his quarter" to read "took his moist array of nickels and pennies." Now we had a contrasting image pattern abuilding. The waitress's fingers are dry, but the coins that came from the cupped hands of the old derelict are moist. By the time Susan finished her additions, she had carried the smeared window slug image to the end of the story where it was repeated in the final paragraph, together with the girl's involuntary revulsion response of wiping her hands on her apron. Finally, Susan made a rather elegant connection between the ant that the girl considered crushing and the "old gentleman." The ant now became "pale brown"—that is, khaki-colored—and the old man's huge trousers became khaki.

Her pattern of linked images was complete. She took the draft home and tinkered with it for another week before submitting the story to the competition. To her great surprise, and my delight, Susan Warne won a prize in that year's literary awards and the story was published in a special edition of the student literary magazine.

Success, as they say, needs no apologists. Susan had learned to use effective imagery as a specific tool to produce the exact tone and mood she intended for her story.

Later, when we discussed her story in class, I introduced a concept that has since proven very helpful. It's what I call the "internal logic of relevant imagery." This sounds quite academic, I'm afraid, but just hang on a minute. I'll try to provide an explanation that's clear and also provides practical craft information. By *internal* logic I mean the two halves of the metaphoric transaction—the two dissimilar objects being compared —are logically connected by the mood goal of the descriptive passage.

The waitress sees the old man as a lower life form, something she can toy with, just as she considered crushing the pale brown ant. Unlike the ant, however, the old man is physically repulsive to her. His moist hands pollute the windows and the cars that he uses for support, and the coins that she, herself, must touch with her clean dry fingers. In her mind, the old man has become an unsavory slug, a creature whom one understandably reviles: the mood goal of the image pattern is revulsion.

So, there is a direct and logical connection between the metaphoric equation: old man = repulsive slug, and the young waitress's mood, which, in turn, sharply reveals her personality. And all this was accomplished without the intervention of a didactic narrator.

Like Susan Warne, you can incorporate this level of sophisticated and relevant imagery patterns in your own work. Do not, however, expect such relatively complex craftsmanship to appear spontaneously in the first draft, or even in the second, for that matter. You have to build such extended relevant images, usually replacing trite patterns and clichés once the main structure of the work is already in place. Admittedly, this is a skill that takes some practice, but the process is certainly not hidden in the impenetrable mists of genius.

Like so many other elements of fiction-writing craft, you begin with Point of View, your sensory filter. Once you've established POV, the reader will absorb the drama through the five senses of the POV character; in other words, the character's human experience will become the experience of the reader. Obviously, mood, one's emotional state at any given time, makes up much of our total human experience. So your character's mood forms an important contribution in meeting the goals of effective dramatic fiction.

Once you know who your protagonist is, and more-or-less what you want the character to experience, and you've assigned well-focused POV, you are ready to develop image patterns that produce the desired mood. This probably will not come easily at first. But, with a few months' practice—using the Fiction Summary and Rewriting Checklist as tools—you'll find yourself writing increasingly elegant patterns of linked images.

At this point, I'd be remiss if I didn't discuss the recurring problem among amateur writers of awkward POV shifts within the same scene. This usually occurs when the writer isn't actually sure what character he wants to be the protagonist. Such shifts often appear in dialogue exchanges:

"We'll have to talk to Dr. Kelly about this," Larry said, trying to control his coiled anger. He scuffed his shoes on the rug and smelled the stale dust and trapped tobacco smoke billowing around him.

"If you think that's really necessary," Mrs. Jamison answered coolly. She could see from the waxy rose tint to his face that he'd been drinking again.

"I sure as hell wouldn't have suggested it if I didn't think it was necessary," Larry shouted. The dust and dead smoke in the overheated room was making him sick. I have to get some air, he thought.

When I read such a shifting POV passage, I realize that the writer won't be able to establish effective mood and tone through linked imagery patterns. Why? Because he is asking his readers to share the moods of two characters simultaneously, thus canceling one with the other.

I know rigid rules are a problem, but here is a strong suggestion. If you want to establish effective mood in a piece of fiction by building images that are conveyed through Point of View, *do not shift the POV from one character to another within the same scene.*

You can have several POVs working in one story or chapter, but give each character his own scene. That way, the reader will be able to absorb the drama (and its supporting mood images) through the sensory filter of a single character at a time, and thus feel he has shared that character's experience.

Now, let's return to the craft process of creating effective mood through logical image patterns.

You've established focused POV, and this has opened for the reader a pathway into the character's mind. At this point, many amateur writers are tempted to use the "he felt, she felt" statement in their efforts to convey character mood. I must caution you against that technique. Almost always, there is a more subtle and elegant way to convey mood than by the direct statement: "Joan felt as angry as she ever had," or, "He felt a rush of sadness," or, "The boy felt fear grip him," etc.

What I suggest to my students is that they use their yellow highlighters or red felt pens to mark all the "he felt, she felt" passages in their drafts, and then to replace these intrusive statements with POV image patterns that dramatize the desired moods.

At first, this may seem a difficult task. But, after a while, you'll come to realize that the overall tone of your work becomes much more professional when you eliminate the intrusive Loudspeaker. In fact, good professional writers rarely resort to such intrusion. They've learned in their apprenticeships that there are better means available.

Let's take the example of scene one of "A Contradiction in Terms," draft number three. Using the Fiction Summary, we ask question one: What am I trying to say about the main character?

For purposes of this argument, the answer is: Martha Phillips becomes so frustrated and angry at Helen Andersen that she loses control, and exposes a violently irrational core beneath her coolly controlled surface.

Now let's examine the image pattern that the author developed as she worked the scene from one draft version to the next. In the first draft, the reader finds Martha dressed in cool blue wool. She smooths the wool and strokes the polished wood of the end table. Martha has just finished waxing the smooth hardwood floor. The stage props connected to Martha all combine to form an image pattern of cool, ordered control, of shiny, sealed surfaces.

Now look at the descriptive passages of Helen. Her book sack is threadbare. Crimson lipstick smears her flesh, and her fingernail has been chewed down to a bloody crescent. Her face is flushed with two manic, unnatural ovals, highlighting the pale skin.

What the reader absorbs here is an image pattern of wounded, vulnerable disorder. Since the POV is firmly focused on Martha, this mood is filtered through her senses. Without the intrusive Loudspeaker proclaiming didactic messages, the reader *feels* the intended contrast of the cool, blue impenetrable Martha with the flushed, bleeding chaos of Helen's life. The author has hit the target mood of the linked images in an elegant and economical manner.

But now look at the second to last paragraph of the scene: "Warm blood rushed to Martha's ears. . . ."

One image—Helen's flushed blood—has now invaded the invulnerability of Martha's icy exterior. Notice that the "warm blood rushed." The word choice here is deliberate. The author had learned that her job was to dramatize change and that she must avoid the clumsy intrusions of the narrator. So, she chose imagery as her device to accomplish this goal.

In the beginning of the scene, Martha is immobile beneath the bloodlessly cool blue shield of her dress. At the end of the scene the stationary chill of her personality has been shattered by an involuntary rush of warm blood. The author effectively dramatized the character change and also rather elegantly foreshadowed the end of the story in which Martha's hot core of violent anger will erupt.

I am not suggesting that this is the work of a Great Author. But I do feel it represents amazing progress by the young writer. When she began the drafts, Ruth was a bright college sophomore, almost totally innocent of professional craft. By the time she completed draft number three, Ruth was using point of view and original metaphor with professional skill to build sophisticated and relevant linked image patterns.

It's important, I think, for beginning writers to understand that they, too, can develop similar habits of professional competence, if they consciously work at their craft formation. Let's briefly examine the process Ruth followed to produce this imagery.

By the end of the first draft, she already had the foundation for the imagery that eventually supported her dramatization of Martha, the protagonist. The cool blue shield of Martha's dress became the kernel of the image pattern that Ruth was to enhance in later drafts. But how, you might ask, did Ruth choose this effective image-core in the first place?

Good question. I don't have an answer, and I'm sure no one else does, either. In my opinion, such fundamental proto-images just jump onto the page from our subconscious minds while we are drafting. That's another reason why I maintain that your first draft is really the raw material of your work. My point is that this linked imagery pattern—Martha's cool, bloodlessly blue emotional shield—existed only as a potential in draft number one. But Ruth had learned to search out and develop such potential images by the time she wrote draft number three.

Teaching fiction writing over the years, I've noticed that there are people who are naturally better at this process than others. Some young writers have a real facility for identifying promising image patterns in their early drafts and skillfully enhancing them as the drafts progress. Others, however, sometimes seem incapable of building effective imagery. I guess this is what some people mean by talent. But I don't believe anyone can produce effective and sophisticated image patterns consistently in first-draft writing, imagery that can simply stand alone without the benefit of the conscious shaping of skilled craftsmanship. Equally, I have repeatedly seen young writers who seemed totally lacking in metaphoric dexterity finish the semester writing fiction that consistently included effective image patterns. It took them much longer than their more talented colleagues, but they eventually developed these craft skills at their own pace.

What I'm suggesting here is that we all seem to have varying amounts of native metaphoric facility lurking beneath our logical consciousness. Some of this will emerge as potential imagery in the early drafts of our stories. But most amateur writers stop the process there. Somehow, they realize, an interesting image has popped up like an exotic mushroom. They are pleased and surprised, but superstitious about tinkering with this *objet d'art*. So that's as far as they take the process.

Professional writers of serious fiction depend on original and effective imagery as a major component of their work. They know that a raw image, still dripping from the subconscious, might *seem* to be the product of dedicated craftsmanship, but they realize that such an artifact is simply the clay, the raw material with which a skilled writer patiently shapes his finished work.

In your own drafts you will discover many similar potential image patterns. If you learn to identify them and to apply your growing skills of craftsmanship to the vital process of building effective and relevant imagery patterns, you will discover that you've gone a long way in your apprenticeship journey toward professionalism.

Professionalism

PART THREE

12

Professional Work Habits
and Attitudes

READING OVER the draft of this book, I realize that I've been unfair to creative writing teachers. Let me emphasize that I consider writing teachers as a group to be about as competent and creative as members of other professions. Just as we have good and bad doctors, lawyers and engineers, we find excellence and mediocrity in similar proportions among writing teachers. I've worked with many energetic and imaginative colleagues who bring to their classes a spirit of exciting creativity. Others have been less vital and inspiring.

But, in my opinion, there is one important component of fiction writing that few full-time teachers can give their students, and that is an understanding of the daily work habits and attitudes that successful professional writers employ as they practice their craft in the competitive real world.

I realize that many who read this book won't need to acquire these work habits or develop the perspective of a professional writer for years. And, of course, many will never need these skills. But, as anyone who has ever tried to quit smoking or go on a salt-free diet can attest, habits build slowly and eventually enter the very fabric of our daily lives. So, now that you have gained an understanding of the fundamental components of effective dramatic fiction, and have absorbed a pattern of related skills that I call the drafting process, you are ready to begin to practice the work habits and benefit from the attitude of a professional writer.

Let me stop here for a moment and clarify an important point. When I talk about professional fiction writers, I mean writers of serious literary-quality fiction, whatever that actually is. I am not talking about Gothic romance, pornography, war fantasy, formula westerns, biker fiction, or glitzy softcore Hollywood epics, à la Sidney Sheldon. You can make a six-figure annual income writing junk fiction, but you sure don't have to learn much craft to do so. In fact, acquiring disciplined craft is probably the last thing you want to do, if you're interested in following in Mr. Sheldon's or Jacqueline Suzanne's illustrious footsteps. So, for the purposes of this book's argument, at least, when I say professional fiction, I mean the kind of story that appears in *The New Yorker, Harpers* or *Esquire,* and the type of novel that finds its way to the front pages of the New York *Times Book Review.*

I think the most important single professional habit a young writer can acquire is daily practice of the drafting process. If you write every day, and apply the logical, disciplined skills of checklist rewriting, you will find your work improving in proportion to the time and concentration you expend.

This might sound easy, but it is not. However, if you break the task down into its component parts, the undertaking is manageable.

Let's look more closely at the practice of daily writing. By this I don't mean that you have to work 365 days each year. But I do suggest that you learn to work slowly and consistently on a draft—be it a short story or a novel—that you chip away at the various draft versions by using daily page or work-time quotas, rather than relying on sudden (and infrequent) storms of inspiration.

In fact, I think that inspiration—like plot and style—is one of those quaint romantic concepts that has little meaning in the career of a professional writer. The cellist in the New York Philharmonic may not be inspired every night she's paid to play, but she still delivers the best performance she can. Equally, you probably won't be motivated to the same degree every day you sit down to work your way through the draft of a short story or novel chapter; I can absolutely guarantee from long experience that you will not be consistently inspired throughout the long process of drafting and rewriting a serious novel. Many days the drafting is easy and fun. Rewriting is rarely either. As the renowned poet John Ciardi describes his own professional habits, "Write hot, but revise cold."

So, you must first learn to approach your daily writing with a sense of controlled resolution. Today, you say, I will draft four pages. Tomorrow, I will draft four pages. By this time next month, my daily quota will rise to five.

Now, that's a noble ambition. After all, by writing five pages a day, six days a week, you can draft a novel manuscript in only three months. Or, using the same pace, you can draft a collection of short stories in this period. But, above all, let's be realistic and practical here. Optimistic fantasy is an endemic affliction of creative people, and overconfidence often collapses into pessimistic depression when one's inflated goals are not reached. Remember this: drafting five double-spaced typewritten pages of serious first-draft fiction involves approximately four hours of uninterrupted concentration. That's equal to about *half* a nine-to-five work day. How can a full-time university student, a full-time accountant, salesperson or homemaker find that much time in a hectic day to concentrate on writing a novel or book of stories?

The answer, of course, is that you will not *easily* find the time to write. If you are to become professional in your work habits, you'll have to learn to restructure your daily life around your writing. And, no matter how you accomplish this restructuring, your "normal" professional life—the work they pay you for—will inevitably suffer, if your writing is to prosper. Moreover, short of quitting your job or your studies and being able to support yourself on some windfall of savings, you'll never have four hours free each day to write five pages.

Therefore, one of the first habits you should acquire is the ability to meet a realistic daily time or page quota. Let's say that you leave the house for work each day at 8:30, and that you normally rise at 7:00. Your regular morning routine involves a shower, the newspaper and breakfast, and half an hour with the "Today Program." In short, the start of your day is a relatively leisurely transition from sleep to professional alertness.

Now, let's see what you could do if you woke one hour earlier, at 6:00. Anybody with reasonable writing skills and a small reserve of motivation can draft two pages of a story or novel chapter in an hour; most of us can draft more than that. Therefore, if you establish a work pattern whereby you wake every day at 6:00, complete your domestic arrangements of bathing and breakfasting in, let's say, forty-five minutes, you have one hour and forty-five minutes free each morning to work. In that period, you should be able to draft about two and a half pages. If you stick to this pattern six days a week, you'll pile up sixty pages a month. In five months, you will have written an average first draft novel manuscript or ten short stories.

I can hear some of you muttering that you simply are not morning people. For you, the best time to work is late at night when everyone else is sleeping. Fine, no problem; I know from my friends that there are, indeed, writers who can only work in the morning and others who must work late in the night. *When* you choose to fill your daily quota is secondary to your commitment to fill it. You may well choose the period between 9:00 P.M. and midnight to work, or even later in the night. What's important is that you are consistent, that you do not allow yourself to be distracted from the task at hand.

And the problem of distraction is a serious threat to a writer's work day. For this reason, I strongly recommend that aspiring professional writers choose early morning to meet their daily drafting quotas. It's unlikely that their family and friends will impose social distractions at 6:45 on a weekday morning.

But, if morning work is simply not practical for you, be rigorous about protecting your evening writing time. This protection involves all the discipline you bring to your "normal" workaday life. For example, if you were down at your office, struggling to complete a quarterly financial report (or its equivalent) and a friend called to invite you out for a pizza or to go fishing (or to go bowling or to the Nicks' game, or whatever), you certainly would not thrust aside your work and happily skip out the office door. Of course, no adult professional would even consider calling another working adult with such an invitation, "Hey, let's skip work today and go watch a movie." Obviously you'll get fired *toute de suite* if you try it. That is not, as they say, a very professional attitude.

But neither is dropping your self-imposed daily time- or page-quota discipline to chat with a friend on the telephone, nor is giving in to the urge to watch Masterpiece Theatre on television. Remember, if you are at your office working on some onerous but necessary task, you cannot simply give up because you'd rather be watching TV or gossiping with your buddies. If you did display such ill-discipline, of course, you'd soon be out of work, a professional failure.

Well, the corollary is that such breaches of professional discipline among writers mean that you will never be able to produce consistently a body of serious, well-crafted work. In other words, without the discipline to thrust aside distractions, you are a dilettante, not a professional.

I know that some readers will feel that they are, indeed, amateurs and not professional writers, and therefore the rigid and rigorous discipline of a daily writing quota is not applicable to their own situation. I would suggest that they examine the professional evolution of musicians for an instructive model.

Anyone who takes piano lessons as a kid soon learns that daily practice is essential for skill formation. Obviously, when we go to a concert hall and hear a skilled professional play a Schubert sonata, we instinctively understand that the virtuosity of the artist is a distillation of lifelong, ongoing discipline. No one would interrupt an aspiring and potentially talented young pianist during his hours of daily practice, nor would such a young performer succumb to the temptation of a trip to the video arcade or a few beers at the corner bar. We take such discipline for granted among musical performers, but we rarely consider the necessity for similar discipline for aspiring professional writers.

So, let us accept as a given that all professional writers must learn self-discipline at some point. For them, the musicians' practice hall is transformed into daily drafting at the writing desk. What happens to the romantic concept of inspiration when faced with the banality of a self-imposed two-page quota? How, you say, can I consistently produce my quota, Monday through Saturday, if I'm not in the mood? The answer is that you must learn to write whether you're in the mood or not. You will be able to draft effective dramatic fiction on a daily basis without dependence on inexplicable and undependable bouts of inspiration, *if* you approach your task with mature professional discipline and employ the fundamental components of the drafting process.

For example, you may find that descriptive metaphor is simply not coming easily on a given day, but that dialogue is a comparative breeze. Well, in such cases, a professional will not simply stop work and wait for metaphor to appear. Instead, he will continue to draft his pages, producing stiff, ineffective metaphor and tight, emotionally moving dialogue. When he piles up the pages of his daily quota, however, he will carefully mark those weak metaphoric sections for particular attention during his redrafting. A week or a month later, when he is moving his draft on to the next version, he'll discover these highlighted weak sections and revise them.

We all have times when one aspect of writing is easier than another. Rarely will we find a day when everything goes well. Yet many young writers refuse to commit themselves to their work unless they experience that euphoric rush of storytelling verve when all components of fiction are perfectly synchronized. This they call "inspiration." I call it romantic nonsense. If you have to wait for some unpredictable seizure of inspiration to occur in order to practice your chosen profession, you're going to have a hard time paying the rent.

So, I think we can agree that daily drafting during the course of any writing project is a desirable professional habit to acquire. But we must not neglect the many practical problems that threaten the application of this habit. First, most of us will want to write at home. That is, we find it most comfortable to establish our daily writing pattern within the private confines of our house or apartment. Many of us, however, do not live alone; we're married or we have roommates or families. Privacy, therefore, is not as accessible as we would prefer. College students, in particular, often have difficulty establishing a permanent writing sanctuary. God knows the rock-blasted warrens of university dormitories are not conducive to the concentration of serious fiction writing. Equally, a homemaker who is distracted by a dinging kitchen timer or a crying child (not to mention the teenager's stereo or the husband's inane Monday Night Football) cannot be expected to concentrate.

So, if you are serious about acquiring professional fiction writing habits, the first task you face is securing a quiet writing office. Notice that I did not use the term "writing studio." This may be empty semantics, but I prefer the word "office" because it connotes diligent discipline, whereas "studio" implies art, and, my old bugaboo, inspiration. An office is a no-nonsense, practical place where you work. And offices are generally efficient.

Now, in the case of a young writer living at home with her family, she need not transform her bedroom into the top floor of IBM headquarters in order to achieve the desired degree of efficiency. But she should establish a quiet, private corner of her room where she can place her writing desk, her draft manuscript and note files, and her typewriter or word processor. Preferably, this small "office" should have a permanent, not a transient feel to it. This is where she works on her quota each day, just as the young pianist goes each day to the same instrument in the same sound-proofed practice cubicle.

All of us will have different opportunities and constraints when it comes to establishing our writing offices. I've worked in almost every conceivable type of place, from a serene whitewashed medieval tower in my first house in Greece, to the basement storage cubical of an overcrowded faculty apartment house in Canton, New York, to the aft cabin of a sailboat in northern Italy. Over the years, I've discovered that serious professional writers employ whatever ingenuity necessary to establish the sanctuary of their own writing office. I've had friends who've converted sheep sheds to offices, and others who have worked in renovated camping trailers. Ernest Hemingway left his cramped Paris apartment each morning with his pencils and *carnets* and sat at the same Montparnasse café table from nine until noon, oblivious to the people around him, drafting and redrafting his stories and novel chapters.

But most of us need a quiet, private corner. This need is especially pressing for college students. I often suggest that they buy a large, cheap briefcase in which they can store their manuscripts, notes and sundry writing materials. This briefcase becomes in effect their office. With it, they can seek out an empty classroom or library study cubicle, close the door, and set up shop for their daily writing session.

Sooner or later, however, most writers will want the relative luxury of a permanent room in which they can arrange their files and notes, set up their typewriter, pace the floor acting out dramatic action and dialogue, read their drafts aloud, and, generally employ all the embarrassing but vital craft components of successful fiction. I know from personal experience that it's difficult to establish such a sanctuary. But I also realize that professional writers always manage to achieve the practical privacy they need.

Once you have found your own sanctuary, and you've learned to structure your day so that you have adequate time to fill your daily quota, you still must overcome several serious obstacles that separate the amateur and the professional writer. One of the biggest problems is what I call "blank page anxiety." This gnawing discomfort (which sometimes flares to panic) is connected to our complex feelings of confidence and our natural fear of failure. All writers experience this anxiety to a greater or lesser degree. It's what we have instead of stagefright. In order to overcome this often crippling affliction, we must first examine the underlying roots of the problem that lie in our own foundation of confidence.

Every writer I've ever encountered (including myself, of course) has basic problems of professional confidence. Either we are crippled with illogical doubts about our ability to *ever* shape this muddled draft into effective fiction, or—equally serious—we are buffeted by illogical overconfidence, a kind of cocaine-rush of grandiosity, a magical euphoria that *every*thing we write today is brilliant.

This emotional see-saw is painful, and after we've experienced it a few times, we become wary about our work, and especially uncomfortable about facing the blank page at the start of our daily writing. Every writer I've ever met has had the same problem, and every successful writer has developed a strategy to combat this anxiety. Often, of course, blank page anxiety leads to crippling procrastination. We seem to grasp *any* distraction, from needless pencil sharpening to cleaning our fingernails, to prevent us from beginning our work, and thus risking failure.

The easiest way I've found to defeat this blank-page panic is to "start" with some words already on the page. I often deface the blank first page of a chapter or story by scrawling an abbreviated outline across the upper lefthand quarter:

Opening:
> Para 1—use dew on deck for POV establishment.
> Para 2—develop fog image.
> Paras 1 and 2—keep dialogue short and low-key.

By marking up the empty page with unnecessary reminders that I've lifted from my outline notes, I find myself less worried about the literary quality of the first-draft passages. In other words, I remind myself yet again that the page will have to be redrafted, that I won't be judged by these imperfect paragraphs so I'm less anxious about the initial flow of words.

Another method many writers use to defeat the terrible white desert of the blank page is to always finish their daily work in the middle of a page. I have employed this technique for fifteen years; obviously, I find it very useful. Normally, I work at my daily quota, until I can see if I'll have time to complete a chapter or scene and to begin drafting the next. If I am almost done with a chapter, for example, I will either finish it and go on to the first page of the next one, or I will stop just short of the chapter conclusion. Sometimes I will stop writing in mid-sentence, so that I can simply pick up in the morning with a modicum of fuss.

I also do not re-read or do my first pencil revisions (or edit-scrolling on the word processor) until the next morning. By withstanding the temptation to pick the scabs of my daily output, I not only review the first-draft pages with a fresh perspective the next day, but I also have a valuable warm-up exercise each morning to get my mind tuned to the next stage of the project.

If you find that any minor distraction tends to interrupt your flow, you may want to try a trick I learned a few years ago. Draft your work on a home-made scroll of 14-inch legal pages, Scotch taped end-to-end. These pages can always be Xeroxed and cut and pasted to form a conventionally sized draft later. But, while you are writing, you escape the distraction of changing pages; also, because the long sheets are taped together, you are less tempted to return to a previous page and become bogged down in compulsive, undirected and premature rewriting—usually a rationalization to avoid plunging into the frightening void of the undrafted story.

If you have an especially severe case of blank-page anxiety, use the carrot-and-stick approach. Choose some pleasant diversion: a cup of coffee, a stroll around the block, ten minutes of watching Nova on PBS, etc. Pause for a moment and mentally savor the pleasures of this distraction. Then tell yourself that you will not accept the pleasant diversion until you complete the scene you're drafting (or the next two pages, or the next paragraph): whatever obstacle you are facing at the time.

This, of course, takes discipline. You simply have to sit there and force yourself to work. For many young writers, such application of will might seem totally alien to the supposedly free and emotionally uplifting creative process. But let me share a secret with you: most writers dislike the actual grind of drafting; it is not fun. What we enjoy is the finished work. To me there is no greater pleasure (including even sex and sailing) than hefting the first copy of a new hardcover book between my sweating palms and staring down at my name printed on the cover. To achieve this goal, I'm willing to put up with all the anxious, lonely drudgery required in the serious process of professional writing.

Conversely, there are many amateur writers who feel that writing must be fun. I'm wary of these people's dedication because I've never met a professional writer who consistently enjoyed the daily slog of drafting serious fiction. These amateurs who wax euphoric about how pleasant it is "to be a writer" are usually involved with the process for social not professional reasons. They become perennial students of evening workshops and devotees of writers' conferences. They buy all the writers' magazines and usually join hometown writers' clubs. In short, they enjoy the accoutrements of the profession, but are unwilling to risk total involvement in the craft, nor, of course, likely to receive the rewards of a professional career.

Before I leave the subject of professional habits and attitudes, I must touch on the usually neglected—and often taboo —area of chemical inspiration: drugs and booze. Over the years there has been considerable nonsense put forth on this subject, especially during the cultural hysteria of the sixties and seventies. Drugs, we were told, would "expand" our minds and inflate our consciousness to cosmic dimensions. During that period young writers sometimes succumbed to the blandishments of Dr. Leary, Richard Brautigan and the other hucksters plying the lucrative TV and campus lecture circuits. From my experience as a writer and a teacher during this period, however, I can attest that those aspiring writers who did attempt to use drugs as a replacement for disciplined craft ended up producing self-indulgent drivel. Their work often had trendy appeal, but no staying power.

By the same token, there has been no shortage of whisky-guru writers proclaiming the creative benefits of hard drinking. Often the mummified image of Ernest Hemingway is held up as an example of the *real* novelist: a macho man who could drink and carouse all night, then churn out brilliant novels in the morning. The reality of this romantic picture, of course, is far different. Hemingway fought a lifelong battle with alcohol; his best work came from those periods of temporary truce with the bottle; his most ludicrous self-parody was the product of his attempting to drink and write simultaneously.

Before you try to enhance your natural writing potential with either alcohol or drugs, ask yourself some fundamental questions. What is the actual writing record—the list of credits —of those writers who proclaim the virtues of cannabis, cocaine or booze? Remember, intoxication is a *subjective* experience. *You* may feel your brain zinging along glittering tunnels of cosmic insight, but it is very doubtful that you will be able to objectively express this experience verbally. Also remember that a hangover—the inevitable price of late-night drinking—dulls the mind to the level of temporary retardation.

As a teacher, I have seen literally scores of potentially talented young writers squander their future careers by embracing the fantasy that they could increase their creativity with chemicals. That, I'm afraid, is an amateur attitude, and unless you eschew it, you will never acquire the disciplined craft of a professional.

On a more optimistic note, let's assume that you have developed the discipline to practice your craft with consistent energy on a daily basis. You are beginning to define yourself as a writer, just as a young musician comes to discover that his life and music have formed an inseparable union. In the next chapter, we will examine how this transformation from amateur to professional operates on the practical level of our daily lives.

13

Professional Planning
and Practices

IN CHAPTER SEVEN, I discussed notetaking and outlining in some detail. Here, I'd like to expand on that subject to include the entire question of scene planning and what I call the writer's "fictional strategy." By this I mean the ongoing internal process during which a successful writer transforms the seemingly mundane mosaic of daily human experience into moving and relevant dramatic fiction. Basically, this strategy involves two elements: attitude and application.

It's been said that the mind of a true musician is rarely free of music. By the same token, most writers think about characters and scenes with varying degrees of intensity during much of their waking lifetime. We tend to daydream fictional scenes; we invent, examine, then retain or discard a variety of fictional characters and scenes while we are driving on the expressway, shopping for spareribs at the Safeway, or waiting at the dentist's office to have a crown replaced.

This active fantasy life is not restricted to fiction writers, of course. Many people find daily solace through private fantasy. And this common fantasy life often takes on a dramatic form. People tell me they see "movies" in their minds, pleasant, often sensual dramas that revolve around their perennial hopes, fears, desires and half-understood life goals.

A woman credit officer at a bank stares at her computer printouts, seeing her eventual life as the owner of a white clapboard bookstore in the shade of palm trees in old town Saint Petersburg. A transmission mechanic at Sears Auto wrestles with a clutch plate, while in his mind he water skis with a beautiful young companion on some untouched turquoise lake in the Canadian Rockies. We all have such inner lives. But only writers *consistently tap* this vein of rich human drama and shape it with their professional craft and discipline.

Let me try to explain how writers make use of the common human impulse to fantasize. First, we develop a deep and readily accessible understanding of fiction's essential core: the dramatic scene. We learn to weave and meld those five fundamental components of the scene . . . relevant setting/situation, POV, action and dialogue, descriptive metaphor and conflict . . . not only into the conscious daily drafting at our writing desks, but also into the more diffuse fantasy stream that emerges from the world around us as we live our daily lives.

We make up stories about the people we encounter every day. Okay, you might say, so what? Everybody makes up fantasies. What's so special about a writer's methods?

The answer is both obvious and complex. Successful writers have practiced their craft long enough to easily sense the *shape* of a potentially effective dramatic scene based on a minimum of initial details. Further, experienced fiction writers have come to empathize very closely with their characters, to crawl inside the skins of their fictional people and to stare out at the world through these characters' eyes. Now, let's say I am planning a short story about Cindy, a fifteen-year-old girl from St. Louis who runs away from the industrial graveyard of the Midwestern Rustbelt with her boyfriend Daryl to the glittery mirage of Los Angeles, where, inevitably, they do not find their dream, and she ends up as a streetwalker on Santa Monica Boulevard.

I know that this Cindy will follow a certain conflict line of scenes from her drab working-class neighborhood, along the old

Oakie trail—now an interstate highway—to the promised land of California. But I am not yet certain what specific domestic conflict will drive her from her home and onto her tragic odyssey with Daryl.

I realize from years of experience, however, that I will discover her motivation if I apply my habitual eavesdropping techniques and combine what I hear with my understanding of the dramatic scene. So, one day I am waiting for my wife on the mezzanine level of a shopping mall in Fairfax, Virginia. It's a Friday evening in December, and the mall's echoing, Muzak-tormented flatlands swarm with shoppers, many of them flushed adolescents, simultaneously trying to shop for Christmas gifts and radiate sexual allure.

Just ahead of me in the sweating hoard are two young girls, obviously Cindy's peers. One wears a shiny satin bomber jacket, the other sports curls like springy brass shavings and elaborate orthodontic braces. They are whispering with theatrical conspiracy.

"She got caught!" the Bomber exclaims.

"The cops?" asks Curly.

"No, her mother. She found the Visa card right in her room, and the, you know, the little blue charge slips."

Curly animates her eyes with mixed delight and empathy for the unnamed girl who seems to have gotten into a jam with a stolen credit card. "What did they do to her?"

But before Bomber Jacket can answer, a hefty Asian woman pushing blond twins in a double-barreled stroller intervenes, cutting off my eavesdropping channel, and almost severing my left big toe. I have, however, heard sufficient evidence. Cindy's domestic tragedy is now clear to me. The scene is building in my mind. It's so *obvious*, why hadn't I understood earlier?

It is late December during the deep recession of the early Reagan years. Cindy, a high school junior in St. Louis, wants to buy Christmas presents for her parents, but she has already lent her meager Burger Chef salary to her boyfriend Daryl so that he can meet the monthly payment on his Mustang. Daryl, it seems, is out of work, but promises to repay her $125 in early January, as soon as he and his brother Jason get their unemployment checks and divide the proceeds of the Christmas tree concession they hope to open—if they can find some more money.

Daryl is a persuasive young man. He convinces Cindy to *borrow* her sister Jeanie's Visa card while she's babysitting and to go to the Cairo State Bank at the Fair Field Mall and there take a cash withdrawal of $200, so that he and his brother can finance their tree concession. At the mall—a setting replete with sweating Muzak-numbed crowds, including a large Asian nanny with sleeping blond twins in a double-barreled stroller— Cindy forges Jeanie's signature and receives the $200 cash advance. But then she succumbs to greed. Why not, she suggests, get another couple of hundred from the Illinois Marine Bank down on the lower level, then throw the Visa card in the trash, as if it had been stolen? Daryl concurs and they rush down the escalator, jostling flushed and weary shoppers on their descent.

But the Marine Bank is no pushover. The thin black woman teller insists on an additional piece of identification beyond Jeanie's 'borrowed' driver's license. Cindy panics; Daryl explodes, calling the teller a "nigger bitch," and the two young people flee into the overheated crowds. In her panic, Cindy has abandoned the Visa card and the driver's license on the cool pseudo-marble counter of the bank.

Dashing through the throngs of shoppers, Daryl realizes that both their faces will have been recorded by the video camera, prominently placed above the teller's glass cubicle. The cops will discover his part in Cindy's forgery. They stumble out of the sweltering mall, into the wind-blasted parking lot. The only course of action they can see is flight. Like so many generations of troubled young Americans before them, Cindy and Daryl head west, toward the hope of anonymous sanctuary and eventual renaissance in California.

I have my opening scene.

> Carol approaches through the hot frustration of the crowds. "Sorry to have taken so long," she says, hefting a bulging Penney's shopping bag in my direction.
> "That's all right," I reply. "It didn't seem very long."

An hour later I was down at my desk, tapping the keys of my word processor, as I blocked out the first scene of the story.

The difference between my fantasy and that of a nonwriter is that I firmly understood that fiction is built on effective dramatic scenes. In addition, I realized that the effectiveness of my characters depended on my ability to capture and utilize the dramatic potential of the working-class ethos of the two kids' world. I had to make my scene both compelling and realistic; I recognized the need to expand mundane reality into fictional drama, avoiding in the process, the temptation of facile melodrama.

So, when I moved in to eavesdrop on the two real-world peers of my adolescent protagonist, I knew that the relatively pedestrian drama involving the unauthorized use of an adult's credit card by one of their peers, could be fictionally transformed through dramatic intensification into the preliminary conflict of my story.

But, more importantly, I also understood that the bare-bones plot conflict of an adolescent girl making a predictably immature mistake would not support my characters on their tragic journey to the commercial sex industry of Los Angeles. There had to be some deeper *human* problem or conflict operating. In this case, I discovered the manipulative and amoral core of Daryl's personality as I fictionally intensified the credit card problem I'd acquired through eavesdropping.

My writer's strategy had once more been successful. When I went to that mall in Fairfax County, Virginia in 1984, I was looking for midwestern teenagers, circa 1981. Because I knew what I needed, I found them. But I did not stop with this unformed nugget of realistic and believable conflict. Instead, I expanded the minor domestic problem between an unnamed mother and a teenage girl into a wider and more sinister fictional conflict. But I retained the gritty, recognizable elements of the suburban shopping mall setting: the stifling Muzak, the crowds, the children dragging mittens on sleeve strings through congealed slush. This became the stage on which Cindy and Daryl could dramatically reveal their personalities and on which the reader could begin to share their human experiences.

What amateur writers can observe in my detailed explanation of this process is the requirement to fictionally expand and intensify real-life characters and conflicts into effective drama, while also avoiding lapses into melodrama. It is often frustrating for me, teaching a Fiction Writing seminar where I encounter students who seem unable to expand events from the real world into believable but compelling dramatic fiction. They either stubbornly insist on replicating bland and interminable conflicts that occur in their daily lives, or, as one writing teacher suggested, they terminate the tepid angst of their scenes with weirdly improbable *deus ex machina* climaxes: a slashing chain saw tumbles inexplicably from a garage shelf (or a blasting shotgun from a jumbled closet) to execute the quibbling couple, thus putting a stop to the weak storyline. In fiction like this, very little happens until the melodramatic conclusion. It is as if the writer is unable to control the actual events in his characters' lives. They are destined to live out the dull weeks and years of the plotline, until, in a fit of terminal boredom, the writer becomes executioner.

Such writers, I believe, lack a serious professional attitude. They seem embarrassed by the fiction writer's craft, as if writing a short story or a novel is, indeed, analogous to telling lies. I will never forget a year-long siege I had with a member of an evening graduate Fiction Workshop I taught at a large mid-western university. Jack was a mature adult, a reporter on the local morning newspaper, a stable, well-adjusted person who often stated that his one ambition in life was to publish a serious novel.

But, unfortunately, Jack already had his novel in first draft form when he came to the workshop. Basically his book concerned a reporter on a city newspaper (a person *very* similar to himself) who becomes a board member on the local United Way fund raising organization. During the course of a relatively uneventful three-month storyline, the protagonist observes various combinations of greed, dishonesty and hypocrisy on the part of his fellow board members, several of whom are community leaders. By the end of the draft, the protagonist resigns from the board in disgust. The revelations of dishonesty and human frailty in the other board members is revealed almost entirely in the protagonist's monologues to a colleague in the newsroom or to his inarticulate lover.

In short, there is very little exploitation of setting/situation to develop compelling dramatic scenes. The protagonist silently observes his flawed peers, then statically reports to uninvolved listeners. Without fully integrated drama, of course, the reader is unable to share any character's human experience. There is no expanding conflict line, and no pivot of illumination.

When I pointed out these structural weaknesses to Jack, he defended his draft in a predictable manner. This is all based on actual events, he explained. *I* was the reporter on the board; the crooked banker and the sanctimonious preacher (a closet homosexual) are drawn from real-world counterparts. There was no need to intensify these characters or their scenes, Jack persisted, because the real people and events were sufficiently compelling without the introduction of "make-believe."

This attitude is, I'm afraid, a common trait, indeed, a touchstone of amateur writers. They seem instinctively to avoid any dramatic modification of people and events that they have either observed in their own lives or about which they've read. In this regard, I occasionally encounter amateur writers of "historical fiction" (Civil War stories, western novels, etc.), who slavishly document their characters authenticity and steadfastly refuse to alter minor historically validated events to fit within dramatically effective scenes.

The underpinning of this attitude, I think, is a basic lack of confidence in the writer's own creative ability. And this self-doubt often seems to have developed in childhood. Whenever I encounter an especially pronounced case of stubborn literal-mindedness, I question the person about his own background of childhood fantasy. Did your parents, I ask, encourage you to cultivate imaginary friends? Did your father and mother make up bedtime stories when you were little? Did they help you expand your own natural powers of imaginative projection, or did they quash such normal childhood fantasy as "silly"?

Almost invariably, the unimaginative would-be writer answers that fantasy, storytelling and mythical domestic playmates were not important aspects of childhood. Among the younger writers afflicted with this disability, I often find that the television set was their childhood companion, their bedtime storyteller. They never learned to enrich the mundane world of domestic existence with myth, with fanciful—fictional, if you will—expansion and intensification. Now, as adults, they are instinctively wary of such trafficking in excess and exaggeration.

It is never too late, I suppose, to change such an attitude, although I feel a writer so afflicted enters his would-be profession with a serious handicap. Most people who want to be writers, however, come from homes where verbal fantasy was part of childhood. But as adults, they usually operate in a world where such active employment of imagination is considered "immature," if not downright unstable. Thus my workshop student, Jack, was unable to separate his professional existence as a factual reporter on the City Desk from his avocational identity as an aspiring novelist. He resisted the imaginative quantum expansion necessary to transform the workaday human conflicts we all see around us into dramatic fiction. In other words, he was unable to envision a believable world where human life is compressed into *scenes.*

If you take nothing else from this book, I would hope that you learn to think of fiction as a progression of effectively rendered dramatic scenes, which are, in turn, composed of carefully exaggerated distillations of the real world. Remember what we said earlier about dialogue: effective dialogue must sound *lifelike,* it must seem to be a believable exchange of the characters involved, but it must never degenerate into a rambling, semi-articulate replication of actual human speech.

Likewise, all the other components of the fictional scene are compressed abstractions of their real-life counterparts. Relevant dramatic action, for example, is an exaggeration of the body language and gesture that is constantly occurring in human interaction. But the dramatic writer is selective: he chooses that which he needs and rejects the remaining myriad elements of real life. This selectivity, the ability to consistently choose relevant detail and to weave it into a dramatic tapestry that convinces the reader's emotions, is, I believe, the true essence of fiction.

And that ability is based in no small part on the writer's attitude, on his confidence to pick and choose, to rearrange the threads of life he observes around him. I need to weave a scene involving a troubled adolescent and her boyfriend. By chance, I encounter two girls on the mundane contemporary byways of a suburban shopping mall. My overall strategic outlook is to opportunistically seize useful snippets of real lives and incorporate them into my fictional cloth. Because my attitude is confident and my foundation of disciplined craft is solid, I can effectively expand on the terse, whispered conversation between Bomber Jacket and Curly. Their unnamed friend's predicament with the misused credit card becomes Cindy's dilemma with her sister's purloined Visa card. I have not actually created the elements of this scene, but I have fictionally altered and intensified the fabric of daily life.

In the process, I have incorporated and integrated other aspects of the shopping mall locale. The demonically repetitive Christmas carols on the Muzak speakers, the oppressive over-heating, the hulking Asian woman careening through the crowd with her two blond twins in their wide-bore stroller—all these elements undergo a sea change into relevant components of my eventual scene.

Because I have acquired the habits of a professional writer —ironic and metaphoric perspective, disciplined notetaking, and the power to retain observed detail and eavesdropped con-versation—and I have learned to incorporate these habits into a pattern of disciplined daily writing, I am able to consistently reshape the mosaic of human existence into effective fictional patterns. If you've ever wondered what writers do with their work day, the above pattern of activity is basically it.

There is no mystery to this process, certainly no genius. Hard work, thoughtfulness and confidence combine to form a professional attitude that leads to successful craft.

There is, however, another vitally important aspect of every successful writer's career that I would be remiss not to examine in some detail. And that is the whole issue of rejection, emo-tional stamina and perseverance.

14

Professional Presentation, Rejection and Perseverance

THE NEXT TIME you're listening to a radio call-in show, note the difference in tone, clarity and voice modulation between the host and the caller. The host always sounds "professional." That is, he does not break his flow of speech with "ah's," "uh's" and "you know's"; his sentences are normally logical declarative statements, and he employs a distinctive tone, a trademark that he's developed over the years to link him to his listeners. In contrast, the caller often sounds confused, inarticulate and nervous.

This same contrast between the skilled professional and the amateur can also be drawn for other groups: actors, photographers, singers, and, of course, writers. One hallmark of a professional is his manner of presentation. Ultimately, of course, the substance of that presentation will decide success or failure—in our case, publishing or rejection. But the general appearance, mechanical correctness and "tone" of one's manuscript submission often combine to prejudge the submission either negatively or positively.

This is only common sense. All across the professional world, there are certain unwritten standards of appearance and attention to detail. Those who truly want to succeed adopt these standards. Conversely, those who do not, are destined to fail.

Working as a journalist, for example, I often find myself in elevators with sales and marketing executives, on their way up to make a presentation at a corporate office. The more important the presentation, the more senior the presenting executive. Being an incorrigible eavesdropper, I overhear conversations among the marketing team. In so doing, several interesting aspects of professional presentation have become clear to me. First, the real pros all dress the part: well-tailored, conservative suits of obvious taste and quality, shoes shined to perfection, hair expertly coifed, fingernails clean and neatly filed. They carry their presentation boards and graphic materials in expensive leather portfolios. As they speak, I've always noted that they have carefully rehearsed the entire presentation, and are simply reviewing their rehearsal in the final moments before the meeting. These professionals radiate confidence.

In contrast, I also encounter struggling young salesmen in these same elevators, kids with chewed fingernails, right out of college on their first professional job. Their rumpled clothes, their overall appearance, their obvious anxiety—even their display boards wrapped in water spotted plastic—all combine to proclaim insecure amateurism.

I realize that this book is about the craft of fiction writing, not marketing and salesmanship. But, when all is said and done, selling a novel or story anthology manuscript to a New York publisher may well be harder than selling an advertising campaign to Campbell Soup.

Industry experts estimate that there are over fifty thousand unsolicited first novel manuscripts delivered "over the transom" each year to New York publishers and literary agents. Indeed, the invention of the Xerox machine, in conjunction with the explosion of creative writing classes across the country, has produced a quantum increase in fiction submissions. Naturally, a similar situation prevails in short fiction submissions to magazines. The competition among fiction writers has never been so severe, and it seems to be getting worse, as the large and upwardly mobile Baby Boom generation matures and seeks outlets for self-expression.

This being the case, any aspiring professional writer has a duty to himself to acquire and practice the manuscript presentation habits of the professional. Initially, this topic might seem of relatively minor importance when compared to the craftsmanship of the work, but the appearance and quality of your submitted manuscript will be your first, possibly your only, contact with a potentially interested agent or editor.

In this discussion, however, I am not going to offer tips about manuscript format and the mechanics of addressing a submission. Opinions vary on this, and you're best advised to simply follow the prevailing pattern suggested in *Writer's Market.* What I mean by "appearance and quality" of a manuscript goes deeper than having your page numbers neatly typed on the upper right-hand corner.

First, you should consider some basic principles. Remember that your manuscript—if it is to be read at all—will be initially scrutinized by a person who is chronically overwhelmed by fiction manuscripts. At many houses, unsolicited submissions are returned unread, but a few are triaged by overworked, poorly paid, and generally harassed young contract readers or editorial assistants, often kids fresh out of school who have managed to secure a precarious clawhold in the ostensibly glamorous world of New York publishing.

Therefore, your manuscript must be relatively *easy* for these screeners to read, i.e., it must be absolutely letter perfect with no typos, misspelled words, grammatical lapses, malapropisms or mechanical errors, such as missing words, etc. I used to suggest to students that the first fifty pages of a novel manuscript display this degree of mechanical perfection. Now I tell them that they're better advised if their *entire* manuscripts are as mechanically flawless as possible.

To this end, I strongly urge every aspiring professional writer to develop his own personal checklist, and to be rigorous in applying the checklist's discipline to his manuscript submissions.

Of course it's difficult to find every misspelled word or typographical error in a 90,000 word typescript, if you rely on eye and brain alone. With a word processor, however, there's no excuse whatsoever for any young writer to submit a manuscript flawed by these minor mechanical errors. I know that many of you instinctively reject the idea of drafting an emotionally evocative story or novel with the chill high-tech equipment of word processing. All right, there's no reason your early drafts of the piece have to be done on a word processor. But your final submission manuscript will benefit considerably if you learn to pass the material through a "user friendly" program like Writing Assistant or Perfect Writer.

The proofreading function of the program will catch *every* misspelled word and every typo. More importantly, the Search function of the program can be tagged to stop each time you've marked a metaphor *mtp* or a verb *vb* or dialogue *dlg*, or at any other tagged element of your draft that you feel bears final examination before printing. In this way, you have the luxury of fine adjustment, of delicate tinkering with extended imagery patterns, of rejecting a neutral verb, or of replacing an overly flamboyant verb with a less evocative Anglo-Saxon generic. The word processing program will handle all the numbing drudgery of searching the manuscript. You are left with your mind and critical powers fresh.

In addition, most good word processing programs will allow you to search a file of draft material for potentially over-used words, names or phrases. With electronic speed, your Writing Assistant will scan your draft and report back that you have used "obviously" sixteen times or "sunburnt" eight times in one scene. A flick of a function key, and you can locate and modify this inadvertent (and very common) awkward repetition.

By adapting your personal rewriting checklist to modern word processing technology, you will raise the overall mechanical level and craftsmanship of your manuscript submission well above the prevailing mediocrity of the manuscript avalanche hitting the mailrooms in New York. A submission that has passed through this final scrutiny-and-correction process will be markedly easier to read than those of the competition. By employing this discipline, you will have gotten an invaluable edge on the scores of thousands of other aspiring writers who are less inclined to adopt new techniques.

Don't misunderstand me here, however. I am not suggesting that the relatively easy mechanical screening available through word processors is in any way a substitute for energetic and imaginative writing. As all computer buffs know, a machine is only as good as its programmer: "Garbage in, garbage out." You can apply all the modern checklist technique in the world to a dull, lifeless draft, a tepid replication of an unexamined life, and what you'll end up with is mechanically clean, attractively presented and ultimately unsuccessful fiction.

Your ability to critically examine your drafts and detect the basic structural flaws of lifeless, unintegrated fiction will probably become your greatest "talent" as a writer. In other words, if you find that your characters simply do not engage each other on an emotionally compelling level in the scenes of a story or novel, you must be as ruthless as a good emergency room doctor in triaging this material. Retain that which is of potential use: the setting, perhaps, or a block of dialogue. Reject the rest and begin your draft again. So many times I have met aspiring writers who bring me a basically flawed manuscript, a novel or story, that they know has structural problems. But when I do my job and indicate these areas of fundamental weakness, and also suggest straightforward methods of salvaging the draft through rewriting, they become irrationally defensive. "I wrote the scene this way because I *wanted* to show Paula alone at the airport before Jean-Claude comes. . . . " Well, she certainly is alone . . . for eight pages, the only person she speaks to is a customs agent.

I remember this and other draft manuscripts so well not because they were "bad," but because they were so potentially good, yet the aspiring writer resisted the only course of action that would lift the draft above the mediocre level. Often such writers will obstinately reject the advice of their teachers and peers and submit a manuscript that they know full well is riddled with structural flaws. To me, this is analogous to appearing at an important interview unprepared, unshaven, and wearing a dirty shirt to boot. "There's a lot of great material in this story," the young writer says in its defense. "A good editor (or a good agent) will see through the problems and recognize my potential."

Maybe. Stranger things have happened on this planet, Lord knows. The chances are, though, that such a clearly flawed submission will be rejected. It may come as a nasty surprise to young writers, but, in my experience, very few editors and even fewer agents still have time to edit or offer critical advice these days. And young contract readers won't last long if they consistently pass on manuscripts that exhibit obvious structural problems for further consideration upstairs.

So, we're back once more to the issue of professional attitude. Please remember what I suggested earlier: a professional is a person who gets paid to avoid mistakes and who practices his craft with consistent skill. If you're flying on United Airlines, you certainly do not expect the captain to start his takeoff roll with a diminished fuel flow clearly indicated in number-two engine. Remember the Air Florida 737 that crashed into Washington's 14th Street bridge? Everyone was deeply shocked at the apparent lapses in professional disciplines by the two pilots. Such laxness was a blatant exception to an industry standard. Usually, we know that we can trust professional pilots.

Well, this degree of professionalism is also found among successful writers of serious fiction. We simply cannot afford to submit sloppy, basically flawed manuscripts—tossed like bread on the waters—and hope for someone else to find and correct our weak points. Of course, errors sneak through, no matter how rigorous we are. But, overall, the manuscripts of successful writers display a much higher level of editing rigor than those amateur manuscripts that find their way back over the transom with the rejection slips.

The choice of what pattern to adopt is entirely yours. I've given you the best advice I have, and you can make your own decisions. Should you choose to retain the romantic attitudes and habits of an undisciplined amateur, that will ultimately be good for me and bad for literature. I'll be forty-six this year, and many of you reading this book are in your twenties. By the time I'm in my sixties, you'll be in your vigorous middle-career years, traditionally a writer's most productive period. If you do adopt the attitude and discipline I've offered in this book, you clearly will be more competition to me in my old age than if you stick with an amateur's methods.

So, as I used to tell my students, "Do me a favor, don't take my advice seriously."

But, even if you insist on learning the craft and habits of a professional fiction writer, you may well never be able to practice your craft professionally. That, I'm afraid, is a cruel reality. As I've tried to indicate, writing requires a long apprenticeship. They say that fewer than ten percent of practicing writers can live on their earnings. In my experience, that may be a high estimate. When you look at other occupations, though, you'll see that only about ten percent of the practitioners are truly expert. How many times have you had an insurance claim or a banking statement fouled up by professional incompetence? I hardly have to mention medical malpractice as a harsh example of eroded professional standards.

The only difference between the mediocre majority in the other professions and writers is that most of these incompetents have an organizational affiliation that continues to protect them —and pay their salaries—during lapses in the profession's standards of excellence. Writers, and all the other individual performers, however, do not have the sinecure and security of corporate affiliation. We have to make our mark anew with each book or story. When we fail, we don't crash as did those two Air Florida pilots, but we do not snatch the brass ring of an advance on royalties either.

For many young writers, though, a rejection slip is almost as devastating as a fatal plane crash. There are probably thousands of amateurs who never recover from their first rejection. Before their submission, they are gripped by such magical conviction that their manuscript will be published, that they send off their one clean copy to a single unknown editor, then sit down on the front porch and begin planning what they're going to wear when Jane Pauley interviews them on the "Today Show." Six months or a year later, when the rumpled, coffee-stained manuscript finally arrives back in Wisconsin or Santa Barbara, the would-be Nobel laureate is so emotionally battered that he vows never again to sell out to the soulless commercialism of New York. If those people don't understand my art, he mutters, it's their loss, not mine.

If you think this is an exaggerated portrait, work a summer writers' conference sometime. Every conference I've ever taught provides at least one embittered novelist who presents his precious manuscript and allows as the *idiots* at Viking, or Knopf, or Dutton, didn't "understand" what he was trying to say. All too often, unfortunately, it's clear that the publishing house understood perfectly well the writer's intention, but found the work fundamentally flawed.

Rather than re-examining the manuscript for major organic problems, however, the writer retreats into a bitter wariness and becomes even more defensive of his book. I suppose that there are equivalents in any performing craft, and that professional musicians or actors are sometimes badgered by failed novices, still seeking magic bullet routes to success. I know that I've encountered more than my share of such angry neophytes.

Occasionally, they end up being legally bled white by the vanity publishers that prey upon such people.

What these failed amateurs never learn is that rejection is an integral part of the writer's apprenticeship. Writing is, after all, a performance, and a manuscript is only one rehearsal version of many possible presentations. If a publisher or agent rejects a submission after giving it adequate reading, it's safe to say that the manuscript has basic problems. It does not necessarily follow that they rejected the book because it simply lacked commercial potential. There is enough of a market for fiction of high literary quality that few publishers would turn down a submission simply because it was too high brow—the standard rationalization of embittered amateurs.

When you plan your submission strategy, it's essential to be prepared for an extremely high rate of rejection. In other words, if you only submit one manuscript at a time, you'll probably grow old before you receive a favorable response. My advice to aspiring writers with a well-crafted first novel or story collection manuscript is to devote as much disciplined effort to the marketing of the book as they did to its writing.

First, they should produce an attractive, letter-quality, letter-perfect typescript that exhibits the highest level of their skill in the early chapters, preferably in the first few pages: a scene or character that will *immediately* seize the professional reader's interest.

Then the writer should have this original or master manuscript professionally reproduced on high grade bond paper, so that it's almost impossible to differentiate between the original and the copies. I know that this process costs money, but so do medical instruments, flight charts, tractors, or any of the other necessary accoutrements of professional life.

Next, use *Writer's Market, Writer's Digest,* or the other industry lists to locate fifteen potential agents and fifteen publishers. It might be more difficult to find the names of the fiction editors at established houses, but, with a little creative deception on the telephone, an imaginative and resourceful person should be able to secure these names.

Now, write your query letters to the editors and agents, enclosing with them a carefully written synopsis of the book, a sample of its most compelling writing, and a brief biographic note on yourself. In this bio note, list your strong points, but don't lie; there are plenty of Janet Cookes out there, and publishing professionals can usually spot them. If you've published in local or student magazines, for example, or won literary competitions, be sure to mention this. If you have studied under a well-known professional writer, get your teacher's permission to use him as a reference in your bio note. Again, make sure that these query letters and their attachments are mechanically flawless and typed on good bond paper. Use embossed letterhead stationary; sign your name with a fountain pen. In short, employ whatever artifice you can to elevate you from the herd of supplicants.

Once you have received some positive replies—maybe as many as two out of fifteen queries—submit your clean manuscript copy and start your waiting clock. If there's no news after seven weeks, call or write the agent or editor to politely prod him to action.

Now, when they do reply with a friendly rejection, as they probably will, try to get them to comment as to the *specific* problems with the draft. Was the beginning too slow (a common problem)? Was the climax unbelievable (another perennial weakness)? Perhaps your protagonist was unlikable, or the dialogue stilted. There are many possibilities. Once you've made contact with a publishing professional, try to benefit from their experience.

Then, armed, we hope, with some clear indication as to the manuscript's weak points, sit down and start correcting them. It should be readily apparent how much word-processing technology can help you at this stage. With the entire draft stored on disks, you can electronically cut and paste and redraft to your ultimate satisfaction, while avoiding the drudgery of retyping an entire new clean draft.

Once you've got the draft restructured, query the original agent or editor again; they just may want to take another peek at it. If not, start the whole process again: fifteen more agents, fifteen more editors, queries and samples, followed by whole manuscript submissions.

This, you might say, seems like a terribly hard job. You're right. But there is no substitute for perseverance, none. If you are to become a successful professional writer, you must learn to accept rejections, to profit from any valid criticism, to rewrite and then to press on with your submission strategy.

Every serious professional writer I know has overcome rejection and gone on to perfect his craft to the point where he can sell his work consistently. Some were luckier than others, but they all learned perseverance along the way. In fact, I strongly believe that perseverance in the face of rejection—not "talent"—is the single most important difference between the successful professional and the failed, embittered amateur. There is horrendous attrition during writers' long apprenticeships. The stubborn survive.

My first year writing in Greece, I knew a fisherman named Stelios. He sailed a little *caique* out of the main bay of Lindos each night for large fish, groupers, sea bass and gray mullet. His technique was simple but exhausting: each hot afternoon, Stelios would bait as many as one thousand hooks, each held by a steel leader in a carefully spaced row to an extremely long drop line. Each night, Stelios would anchor his kilometer-long array of baited hooks in likely water. Then, at dawn he would return, locate his white plastic marker float and haul in the heavy dripping line. Usually, smaller fish would have stolen the bait from the thumb-thick hooks, leaving the barb bare. Many times, he had nothing to show for his efforts. Some mornings, however, he would land a thrashing five-kilo *synagrita* or hulking brown grouper.

Then he would sell his catch to the restaurant on the beach, buy some fuel for his boat and maybe a cold bottle of Fix beer for himself, then hunker down in the baking summer sun to recoil and rebait his long hook line.

I once asked him if he wouldn't prefer an easier life. Other fishermen took out tourists in their boats, I explained, and they made considerably more money without such frustrating and exhausting labor.

Stelios squinted up from the rusty boards of his foredeck, the thick nylon line gripped by a stubby, sun-black toe and the leather flipper of his right hand. *"Etsi,"* he said. "Fishing is a hard life. But . . . *ti na kanome,* what can I do?" He turned slowly to take in the walls of the Lindos acropolis, the whitewashed village, and the morning sea. "I am a fisherman," he said with slow dignity. "I fish."

I gestured down at the tangled coil of the hook line. "But your life is so difficult," I persisted. "Isn't there an easier way?"

"Twenty-six years I've been going out in my boat," Stelios answered. "Never once have I seen a fish commit suicide by leaping on my deck." He grinned now, exposing his one gold tooth and his missing canine. "If I don't bait my hooks each day, no one else will. It's hard work, but it's what I do." Again, he squinted at the quiet morning sea, remembering, perhaps, dark storms. "I am a fisherman," he repeated with sudden passion.

When I finish editing this manuscript and complete all the drudgery of proofreading, and before I begin the endless verbal line coiling of the next book, I will go up to a Greek restaurant on Baltimore harbor and drink one thimble glass of ouzo in tribute to Stelios, who taught me perseverance, and one shot of pale golden tequilla to the late John Gardner, who, four winters ago on a smoky night in Ciudad Juarez, convinced me to write this book.

March 1985
Washington, DC

Practical
Appendices

PART FOUR

THESE APPENDICES are meant to serve as practical tools in your daily work as fiction writers. They are not sacred dogma, but suggested guidelines. Over the years, teaching and writing, I've discovered that a writer—myself included—can benefit from straight-forward and accessible reminders of craft components. There are many elements in successful fiction, and the drafting process is a complex sequence. These guidelines, then, are meant to serve as sign posts along your route. If you already know the way, you may choose to ignore them. However, when you're feeling lost among the maze of metaphor, characters and dialogue, you may wish to consult this road map.

I. The Function and Requirements of Physical Setting and Conflict Situation

1. Function of Setting

Physical setting and the emotional situation of characters within that setting has a direct relationship to conflict development.

Examine your possible setting/situations for dramatic potential:

Can my protagonist and the important supporting character(s) believably interact in this setting/situation?

Can the conflict of the storyline economically progress on this "stage" to a Pivot of Illumination, or must I shift setting several times before reaching that point?

Are there sufficient setting details (stage props) to help dramatize my characters' emotions without resorting to gratuitous "cigarette action"?

2. Requirements of Setting

Can I draw a believable setting? Do I have enough evocative detail, i.e. objects, fixtures, street names, etc.?

What specific research must I do to construct a believable setting?

Is there a believable relationship between the character's background and identity and the setting/situation?

Can I create the setting economically through POV at the start of the scene?

II. The Function and Requirements of Point of View: The Sensory Filter

1. *Function of POV*

Because the purpose of serious fiction is to provide a shared human experience, Point of View is one of your strongest dramatic tools, analogous to the "close-up" in film. Once the reader can experience the fictional world through the five senses of the protagonist, he will be better able to empathize, to share that character's experience.

By establishing POV early in each scene, the reader can easily identify the protagonist.

With tightly focused POV, the reader can sense the character's mood changes without the clumsy intrusion of the Loudspeaker Narrator (a clear indication of amateur technique).

Closely focused POV allows for a *direct* connection between imagery patterns and character mood: see "At the Tel-way" for examples of this: hand smear on the window = implied slime trail of slug = mood of repulsion.

212 / Practical Appendices

2. Requirements of POV

Use all five senses when convenient, not simply sight.

Avoid overuse of POV "tags": "He saw." "She could hear." "John felt the rough edge," etc. Use, instead, direct sensation, i.e.: "The humid night was sharp with mildew. Heat pulsed from the spongy tarmac beneath his boot soles. He was back in Vietnam."

Do not pointlessly shift Point of View from one character to another within the same scene. This awkward POV shifting is one of the most common problems of beginning writers and a clear indicator of amateur technique.

Once POV is established, you can enter the character's thoughts through direct monologue without resorting to clumsy tags, i.e., "She thought," "He realized," etc.

POV should be most tightly focused at *pivotal* points of your scenes.

III. The Function and Requirements of Dialogue

1. *The Function of Dialogue*

Dialogue gives flavor to a character. Speech patterns show emotional state, regional, ethnic and educational background. Dialogue is an important tool in establishing *character identity.* Your characters' dialogue should have an individual ring; employ repeated slang or speech patterns by certain characters, but do not go overboard.

Dialogue can move storyline (plot) ahead economically. For example, a character can announce that she has reached a decision and that her counterpart will not like what she has to say. This immediately heightens the level of conflict without the Loudspeaker Narrator didactically proclaiming the nature of the problem. In a similar manner, dialogue can refer to past events that provide necessary background information very economically. However, you must be wary of "Bob and Ray" dialogue here.

Dialogue is often used in foreshadowing. But you must be careful not to slip into archaic Dickensian tone.

2. *The Requirements of Dialogue*

Dialogue must *sound believable;* it must be in character. Remember, we all employ contractions and generic nouns when we speak: "Why don't we go downtown and try that new French place they're all talking about?" In dialogue, children speak like children, adults like adults, etc. But do not attempt to replicate human speech, with all its inarticulate pauses and social posturing. Dialogue must be a dramatic, compressed exaggeration of natural speech.

Dialogue must be a believable exchange of information between the characters involved. Never resort to "Bob and Ray" dialogue in which characters tell each other obvious background information simply for the reader's benefit:

"Yes, Mary, we've been married ten years now. It's funny, thinking back how we met in college, and how your parents disliked me because I was poor, and because I wasn't even a citizen then. But now, I'm District Attorney, and your dad comes to me all the time for favors."

That is "Bob and Ray" dialogue, a hallmark of amateur writing.

Dialogue must have some *purpose* in furthering character or conflict development. Do not use dialogue simply as a filler. Also, do not use dialogue as unnecessary "connective tissue" transition:

"Do you want to go to the beach today?"

"I don't know, do you?"

"Yeah, maybe. I'll make some sandwiches. You get the car."

"Okay."

Instead of this transition from one scene to the next—what is known as moving the character from Point A to Point B— simply cut one scene at a pivotal point, use a four-space break with asterisks.

IV. The Function and Requirements of Dramatic Action

1. Function of Dramatic Action

People normally reflect their feeling by what they do: gesture, expression and body language. This is non-verbal communication, every bit as important in drama as dialogue. In stage or film drama, the characters emote through obvious action and gesture. In fiction, the writer must provide similar action, but on a slightly reduced level.

Often this dramatic action will appear as a gesture or movement that takes the place of or supplements a dialogue tag:

"Well, I don't know," Larry said, gnawing at the shredded remnant of his fingernail, "Do you *really* want to go tonight?"

This action obviously reflects the character's anxiety, without the Loudspeaker Narrator resorting to a proclamation about Larry's emotional state.

Dramatic action can serve as an economical method of providing a character's background information. For example, if we find a young man working in a garage, quietly enjoying the task of stripping down an automatic transmission, we can assume that he's a skilled mechanic.

Dramatic action (Martha Phillips reading her philosophy text) often combines with stage props to dramatize mood and character identity.

Dramatic action can foreshadow. If a scene opens with Larry, the young auto mechanic, carefully shaving, then dressing in an expensive suit, the reader knows that he is preparing for an unusual activity. In this case, he's going to the party he actually wants to avoid. The writer does not dramatize *every* action of his preparation, but instead selects *relevant* actions that will show his anxiety. Perhaps he has trouble with his necktie, or his cufflinks; maybe he smears his cuff when he tries to buff his shoe. Here, the action serves to dramatize character mood, not to replicate real life.

As with dialogue, dramatic action and gesture is an *exaggerated compression* of the actual world.

2. The Requirements of Dramatic Action

Dramatic action must serve some purpose in furthering character development or storyline. Use your checklist to avoid gratuitous "cigarette action."

Dramatic action should appear lifelike and natural to the character. Focus on certain *critical* moments that reveal characters' moods and anxieties.

Use dramatic action with POV and stage props to provide a focused human experience.

v. The Function and Requirements
of Metaphor and Image

1. The Function of Metaphor

Metaphor is not simply a pretty decoration. Metaphor need not be pleasant. The function of metaphor is to evoke emotions in both the character and, through him, the reader. Therefore, metaphor must carry emotional impact.

To be emotionally evocative, metaphor must be original. Trite description and cliché do not evoke emotions.

Descriptive metaphor, when coupled with Point of View, will serve to reveal the character's mood. For example: "He rolled up the moldy curtain of the compartment window and gazed at the green rain. Overhead the sky hunkered lower, wet concrete above the dead palms."

For a character to perceive monsoon clouds as "wet concrete" reveals an underlying depression, an anxiety.

Metaphor often combines into *image patterns*. When Martha Phillips sees Helen Andersen's desk as a "wrecked truck" and the half-eaten Twinkie as "mummified," the reader receives an emotional message of waste, destruction and chaos.

2. The Requirements of Metaphor and Image

Metaphoric language must be original and relevant to character mood.

A serious writer will locate and correct *all* trite descriptions and cliché on a draft before proceeding to the next draft version.

Experienced writers will alternate harsh and pleasant metaphor, depending on character mood.

Metaphor should be coupled with POV and relevant stage props, not "pasted on" like a smile-face decal. Remember, gratuitous metaphor is a sign of amateur writing.

VI. The Personal Rewriting Checklist

THIS LIST IS, indeed, personal. No two writers will need the same list, but we can all profit from using one that is tailored to our particular needs. When you write your own, be ruthless with yourself. If, for example, you tend to overuse a certain word or phrase . . . "dazzling" or "He turned slowly and . . . " add this problematic language to your checklist. It might seem awkward, but you will avoid these repetitions, and soon, you will no longer need to refer to that item. Remember, the checklist is a *practical* writing tool, not a piece of literary theory. You should consider your checklist as flexible; add to it or delete as required. But be sure to use it between the first and second draft. You will be truly amazed how dramatically the quality of your work improves.

SAMPLE PERSONAL REWRITING CHECKLIST

Scene =
(reminder)

- Believable and Relevant Setting / Situation
- Point of View (established early and maintained on one character only in each scene)
- Problem or Conflict (established as early as practical)
- Relevant Dramatic Action (no "cigarette action")
- Relevant Dialogue (no "Bob and Ray dialogue)
- Relevant Metaphor and Image (no clichés)

* * *

Read all drafts aloud for awkward repetitions of words and phrases.

Write Story Intention as a statement.

Does setting relate to character?

Are stage props relevant?

What is the dramatic potential of my setting?

Who is main character? Is he/she identified through POV?

Where is POV established?

Does POV shift?

Is POV reinforced? If so, why?

When does conflict first appear? Soon enough?

Is dramatic physical action connected to characters' mood?

Does Dialogue fulfill its Functions and Requirements?

Does Physical Action fulfill its Functions and Requirements?

No "Bob and Ray" Dialogue?

No "Cigarette Action"?

Is Dialogue supported by relevant action / gesture?

Any awkward and irrelevant dialogue tags?

Check for clichés.

Check, *again*, for clichés.

Ask someone else to check for clichés.

Are minor characters sufficiently *exaggerated* through action, dialogue and stage props to give them identity (Large Asian woman with double-barrelled stroller)?

Are my VERBS relevant to the situation? Do I really want a neutral Anglo-Saxon generic here, or do I prefer a more evocative verb? And vice versa?

Have I developed linked image patterns to create a mood?

Have I experimented with other metaphors?

Can I locate the Pivot of Illumination or emotional change?

Read second draft aloud.

Repeat checklist for second draft.

Tag problem areas: dialogue, verbs, metaphors, etc., for word processor final editing / proofreading.

Suggested Reading

How to Write and Publish Your Novel, by William Knott, Reston, VA: Reston Publishing Company, 1982.

On Writing Well, by Willia Zinsser, New York: Harper & Row Publishers, Inc., 1980.

The Art of Fiction, by John Gardner, New York: Alfred A. Knopf, Inc., 1984.

The Craft of Writing, by William Sloane, New York: W.W. Norton & Co., Inc., 1979.

The Elements of Style, by William Strunk, Jr., and E. B. White, New York: Macmillan, 1979.

Writer's Market, Cincinnati, OH: Writer's Digest, annually.